A Fragment of Life

Other books by Arthur Machen

Novels

The Hill of Dreams
The Great Return
The Terror
The Secret Glory
The Green Round
The Great God Pan
Kings of Horror
The Chronicle of Clemendy
The Great God Pan and The Inmost Light
The Three Imposters
The House of Souls
The Angels of Mons, The Bowmen,
      and Other Legends of the War
Fantastic Tales or the Way to Attain
The Shining Pyramid
The Glorious Mystery
Ornaments in Jade
The Children of the Pool and Other Stories
The Cozy Room and Other Stories
Holy Terrors
Tales of Horror and the Supernatural
Tales of Horror and the Supernatural Volume Two
The Strange World of Arthur Machen
Black Crusade
The Novel of the Black Seal and Other Stories
The Novel of the White Powder and Other Stories

A Fragment of Life

Arthur Machen

ÆGYPAN PRESS

A Fragment of Life
A publication of
ÆGYPAN PRESS

www.aegypan.com

I

Edward Darnell awoke from a dream of an ancient wood, and of a clear well rising into grey film and vapor beneath a misty, glimmering beat; and as his eyes opened he saw the sunlight bright in the room, sparkling on the varnish of the new furniture. He turned and found his wife's place vacant, and with some confusion and wonder of the dream still lingering in his mind, he rose also, and began hurriedly to set about his dressing, for he had overslept a little, and the 'bus passed the corner at 9:15. He was a tall, thin man, dark-haired and dark-eyed, and in spite of the routine of the City, the counting of coupons, and all the mechanical drudgery that had lasted for ten years, there still remained about him the curious hint of a wild grace, as if he had been born a creature of the antique wood, and had seen the fountain rising from the green moss and the grey rocks.

The breakfast was laid in the room on the ground floor, the back room with the French windows looking on the garden, and before he sat down to his fried bacon he kissed his wife seriously and dutifully. She had brown hair and brown eyes, and though her lovely face was grave and quiet, one would have said that she might have awaited her husband under the old trees, and bathed in the pool hollowed out of the rocks.

They had a good deal to talk over while the coffee was poured out and the bacon eaten, and Darnell's egg brought in by the stupid, staring servant-girl of the dusty face. They had been married for a year, and they had got on excellently, rarely sitting silent for more than an hour, but for the past few weeks Aunt Marian's present had afforded a subject for conversation which seemed inexhaustible. Mrs. Darnell had been Miss Mary Reynolds, the daughter of an auctioneer and estate agent in Notting Hill, and Aunt Marian was her mother's sister, who was supposed rather to have lowered herself by marrying a coal merchant, in a small way, at Turnham Green. Manan had felt the family attitude a good deal, and the Reynoldses were sorry for many things that had been said, when the coal merchant saved money and took up land on building leases in the neighborhood of Crouch End, greatly to his advantage, as it appeared. Nobody had thought that Nixon could ever do very much; but he and his wife had been living for years in a beautiful house at Barnet, with bow-windows, shrubs, and a paddock, and the two families saw but little of each other, for Mr. Reynolds was not very prosperous. Of course, Aunt Marian and her husband had been asked to Mary's wedding, but they had sent excuses with a nice little set of silver apostle spoons, and it was feared that nothing more was to be looked for. However, on Mary's birthday her aunt had written a most affectionate letter, enclosing a check for a hundred pounds from "Robert" and herself, and ever since the receipt of the money the Darnells had discussed the question of its judicious disposal. Mrs. Darnell had wished to invest the whole sum in Government securities, but Mr. Darnell had pointed out that the rate of interest was absurdly low, and after a good deal of talk he had persuaded his wife to put ninety pounds of the money in a safe mine, which was paying five percent. This was very well, but the remaining ten pounds, which Mrs. Darnell had insisted on reserving, gave rise to legends and discourses as interminable as the disputes of the schools.

At first Mr. Darnell had proposed that they should furnish the "spare" room. There were four bedrooms in the house: their own room, the small one for the servant, and two others overlooking the garden, one of which had been used for storing boxes, ends of rope, and odd numbers of "Quiet Days" and "Sunday Evenings," besides some worn suits belonging to Mr. Darnell which had been carefully wrapped up and laid by, as he scarcely knew what to do with them. The other room was frankly waste and vacant, and one Saturday afternoon, as he was coming home in the 'bus, and while he revolved that difficult question of the ten pounds, the unseemly emptiness of the spare room suddenly came into his mind, and he glowed with the idea that now, thanks to Aunt Marian, it could be furnished. He was busied with this delightful thought all the way home, but when he let himself in, he said nothing to his wife, since he felt that his idea must be matured. He told Mrs. Darnell that, having important business, he was obliged to go out again directly, but that he should be back without fail for tea at half-past six; and Mary, on her side, was not sorry to be alone, as she was a little behind-hand with the household books. The fact was, that Darnell, full of the design of furnishing the spare bedroom, wished to consult his friend Wilson, who lived at Fulham, and had often given him judicious advice as to the laying out of money to the very best advantage. Wilson was connected with the Bordeaux wine trade, and Darnell's only anxiety was lest he should not be at home.

However, it was all right; Darnell took a tram along the Goldhawk Road, and walked the rest of the way, and was delighted to see Wilson in the front garden of his house, busy amongst his flower-beds.

"Haven't seen you for an age," he said cheerily, when he heard Darnell's hand on the gate; "come in. Oh, I forgot," he added, as Darnell still fumbled with the handle, and vainly attempted to enter. "Of course you can't get in; I haven't shown it you."

It was a hot day in June, and Wilson appeared in a costume which he had put on in haste as soon as he arrived from the City. He wore a straw hat with a neat pugaree protecting the back of his neck, and his dress was a Norfolk jacket and knickers in heather mixture.

"See," he said, as he let Darnell in; "see the dodge. You don't *turn* the handle at all. First of all push hard, and then pull. It's a trick of my own, and I shall have it patented. You see, it keeps undesirable characters at a distance — such a great thing in the suburbs. I feel I can leave Mrs. Wilson alone now; and, formerly, you have no idea how she used to be pestered."

"But how about visitors?" said Darnell. "How do they get in?"

"Oh, we put them up to it. Besides," he said vaguely, "there is sure to be somebody looking out. Mrs. Wilson is nearly always at the window. She's out now; gone to call on some friends. The Bennetts' At Home day, I

think it is. This is the first Saturday, isn't it? You know
J. W. Bennett, don't you? Ah, he's in the House; doing
very well, I believe. He put me on to a very good thing
the other day."

"But, I say," said Wilson, as they turned and strolled
toward the front door, "what do you wear those black
things for? You look hot. Look at me. Well, I've been
gardening, you know, but I feel as cool as a cucumber.
I dare say you don't know where to get these things?
Very few men do. Where do you suppose I got 'em?"

"In the West End, I suppose," said Darnell, wishing
to be polite.

"Yes, that's what everybody says. And it is a good cut.
Well, I'll tell you, but you needn't pass it on to everybody. I got the tip from Jameson — you know him,
'Jim-Jams,' in the China trade, 39 Eastbrook — and he
said he didn't want everybody in the City to know
about it. But just go to Jennings, in Old Wall, and
mention my name, and you'll be all right. And what
d'you think they cost?"

"I haven't a notion," said Darnell, who had never
bought such a suit in his life.

"Well, have a guess."

Darnell regarded Wilson gravely.

The jacket hung about his body like a sack, the
knickerbockers drooped lamentably over his calves,
and in prominent positions the bloom of the heather
seemed about to fade and disappear.

"Three pounds, I suppose, at least," he said at length.

"Well, I asked Dench, in our place, the other day,
and he guessed four ten, and his father's got something
to do with a big business in Conduit Street. But I only
gave thirty-five and six. To measure? Of course; look at
the cut, man."

Darnell was astonished at so low a price.

"And, by the way," Wilson went on, pointing to his

new brown boots, "you know where to go for shoe-leather? Oh, I thought everybody was up to that! There's only one place. 'Mr. Bill,' in Gunning Street, — nine and six."

They were walking round and round the garden, and Wilson pointed out the flowers in the beds and borders. There were hardly any blossoms, but everything was neatly arranged.

"Here are the tuberous-rooted Glasgownias," he said, showing a rigid row of stunted plants; "those are Squintaceæ; this is a new introduction, Moldavia Semperflorida Andersonii; and this is Prattsia."

"When do they come out?" said Darnell.

"Most of them in the end of August or beginning of September," said Wilson briefly. He was slightly annoyed with himself for having talked so much about his plants, since he saw that Darnell cared nothing for flowers; and, indeed, the visitor could hardly dissemble vague recollections that came to him; thoughts of an old, wild garden, full of odors, beneath grey walls, of the fragrance of the meadowsweet beside the brook.

"I wanted to consult you about some furniture," Darnell said at last. "You know we've got a spare room, and I'm thinking of putting a few things into it. I haven't exactly made up my mind, but I thought you might advise me."

"Come into my den," said Wilson. "No; this way, by the back"; and he showed Darnell another ingenious arrangement at the side door whereby a violent high-toned bell was set pealing in the house if one did but touch the latch. Indeed, Wilson handled it so briskly that the bell rang a wild alarm, and the servant, who was trying on her mistress's things in the bedroom, jumped madly to the window and then danced a hysteric dance. There was plaster found on the drawing room table on Sunday afternoon, and Wilson wrote a letter to the "Fulham Chronicle," ascribing the phenomenon "to some disturbance of a seismic nature."

For the moment he knew nothing of the great results of his contrivance, and solemnly led the way toward the back of the house. Here there was a patch of turf, beginning to look a little brown, with a background of shrubs. In the middle of the turf, a boy of nine or ten was standing all alone, with something of an air.

"The eldest," said Wilson. "Havelock. Well, Lockie, what are ye doing now? And where are your brother and sister?"

The boy was not at all shy. Indeed, he seemed eager to explain the course of events.

"I'm playing at being Gawd," he said, with an engaging frankness. "And I've sent Fergus and Janet to the bad place. That's in the shrubbery. And they're never to come out anymore. And they're burning forever and ever."

"What d'you think of that?" said Wilson admiringly. "Not bad for a youngster of nine, is it? They think a lot of him at the Sunday-school. But come into my den."

The den was an apartment projecting from the back of the house. It had been designed as a back kitchen and washhouse, but Wilson had draped the "copper" in art muslin and had boarded over the sink, so that it served as a workman's bench.

"Snug, isn't it?" he said, as he pushed forward one of the two wicker chairs. "I think out things here, you know; it's quiet. And what about this furnishing? Do you want to do the thing on a grand scale?"

"Oh, not at all. Quite the reverse. In fact, I don't know whether the sum at our disposal will be sufficient. You see the spare room is ten feet by twelve, with a western exposure, and I thought if we *could* manage it, that it would seem more cheerful furnished. Besides, it's pleasant to be able to ask a visitor; our aunt, Mrs. Nixon, for example. But she is accustomed to have everything very nice."

"And how much do you want to spend?"

"Well, I hardly think we should be justified in going much beyond ten pounds. That isn't enough, eh?"

Wilson got up and shut the door of the back kitchen impressively.

"Look here," he said, "I'm glad you came to me in the first place. Now you'll just tell me where you thought of going yourself."

"Well, I had thought of the Hampstead Road," said Darnell in a hesitating manner.

"I just thought you'd say that. But I'll ask you, what is the good of going to those expensive shops in the West End? You don't get a better article for your money. You're merely paying for fashion."

"I've seen some nice things in Samuel's, though. They get a brilliant polish on their goods in those superior shops. We went there when we were married."

"Exactly, and paid ten percent more than you need have paid. It's throwing money away. And how much did you say you had to spend? Ten pounds. Well, I can tell you where to get a beautiful bedroom suite, in the very highest finish, for six pound ten. What d'you think of that? China included, mind you; and a square of carpet, brilliant colors, will only cost you fifteen and six. Look here, go any Saturday afternoon to Dick's, in the Seven Sisters Road, mention my name, and ask for Mr. Johnston. The suite's in ash, 'Elizabethan' they call it. Six pound ten, including the china, with one of their 'Orient' carpets, nine by nine, for fifteen and six. Dick's."

Wilson spoke with some eloquence on the subject of furnishing. He pointed out that the times were changed, and that the old heavy style was quite out of date.

"You know," he said, "it isn't like it was in the old days, when people used to buy things to last hundreds of years. Why, just before the wife and I were married, an uncle of mine died up in the North and left me his furniture. I was thinking of furnishing at the time, and I thought the things might come in handy; but I assure you there wasn't a single article that I cared to give houseroom to. All dingy, old mahogany; big bookcases and bureaus, and claw-legged chairs and tables. As I said to the wife (as she was soon afterward), 'We don't exactly want to set up a chamber of horrors, do we?' So I sold off the lot for what I could get. I must confess I like a cheerful room."

Darnell said he had heard that artists liked the old-fashioned furniture.

"Oh, I dare say. The 'unclean cult of the sunflower,' eh? You saw that piece in the 'Daily Post?' I hate all that rot myself. It isn't healthy, you know, and I don't believe the English people will stand it. But talking of curiosities, I've got something here that's worth a bit of money."

He dived into some dusty receptacle in a corner of the room, and showed Darnell a small, worm-eaten Bible, wanting the first five chapters of Genesis and the last leaf of the Apocalypse. It bore the date of 1753.

"It's my belief that's worth a lot," said Wilson. "Look at the worm-holes. And you see it's 'imperfect,' as they call it. You've noticed that some of the most valuable books are 'imperfect' at the sales?"

The interview came to an end soon after, and Darnell went home to his tea. He thought seriously of taking Wilson's advice, and after tea he told Mary of his idea and of what Wilson had said about Dick's.

Mary was a good deal taken by the plan when she had heard all the details. The prices struck her as very moderate. They were sitting one on each side of the grate (which was concealed by a pretty cardboard screen, painted with landscapes), and she rested her cheek on her hand, and her beautiful dark eyes seemed to dream and behold strange visions. In reality she was thinking of Darnell's plan.

"It would be very nice in some ways," she said at last. "But we must talk it over. What I am afraid of is that it will come to much more than ten pounds in the long run. There are so many things to be considered. There's the bed. It would look shabby if we got a common bed without brass mounts. Then the bedding, the mattress, and blankets, and sheets, and counterpane would all cost something."

She dreamed again, calculating the cost of all the necessaries, and Darnell stared anxiously; reckoning with her, and wondering what her conclusion would be. For a moment the delicate coloring of her face, the grace of her form, and the brown hair, drooping over her ears and clustering in little curls about her neck, seemed to hint at a language which he had not yet learned; but she spoke again.

"The bedding would come to a great deal, I am afraid. Even if Dicks are considerably cheaper than Boons or Samuels. And, my dear, we must have some ornaments on the mantelpiece. I saw some very nice vases at eleven-three the other day at Wilkin and Dodd's. We should want six at least, and there ought to be a center-piece. You see how it mounts up."

Darnell was silent. He saw that his wife was summing up against his scheme, and though he had set his heart on it, he could not resist her arguments.

"It would be nearer twelve pounds than ten," she said.

"The floor would have to be stained round the carpet (nine by nine, you said?), and we should want a piece of linoleum to go under the washstand. And the walls would look very bare without any pictures."

"I thought about the pictures," said Darnell; and he spoke quite eagerly. He felt that here, at least, he was unassailable. "You know there's the 'Derby Day' and the 'Railway Station,' ready framed, standing in the corner of the box-room already. They're a bit old-fashioned, perhaps, but that doesn't matter in a bedroom. And couldn't we use some photographs? I saw a very neat frame in natural oak in the City, to hold half a dozen, for one and six. We might put in your father, and your brother James, and Aunt Marian, and your grandmother, in her widow's cap — and any of the others in the album. And then there's that old family picture in the hair-trunk — that might do over the mantelpiece."

"You mean your great-grandfather in the gilt frame? But that's *very* old-fashioned, isn't it? He looks so queer in his wig. I don't think it would quite go with the room, somehow."

Darnell thought a moment. The portrait was a "kit-cat" of a young gentleman, bravely dressed in the fashion of 1750, and he very faintly remembered some old tales that his father had told him about this ancestor — tales of the woods and fields, of the deep sunken lanes, and the forgotten country in the west.

"No," he said, "I suppose it is rather out of date. But I saw some very nice prints in the City, framed and quite cheap."

"Yes, but everything counts. Well, we will talk it over, as you say. You know we must be careful."

The servant came in with the supper, a tin of biscuits, a glass of milk for the mistress, and a modest pint of beer for the master, with a little cheese and butter. Afterward Edward smoked two pipes of honeydew, and they went quietly to bed; Mary going first, and her husband following a quarter of an hour later, according to the ritual established from the first days of their marriage. Front and back doors were locked, the gas was turned off at the meter, and when Darnell got upstairs he found his wife already in bed, her face turned round on the pillow.

She spoke softly to him as he tame into the room.

"It would be impossible to buy a presentable bed at anything under one pound eleven, and good sheets are dear, anywhere."

He slipped off his clothes and slid gently into bed, putting out the candle on the table. The blinds were all evenly and duly drawn, but it was a June night, and beyond the walls, beyond that desolate world and wilderness of grey Shepherd's Bash, a great golden moon had floated up through magic films of cloud, above the hill, and the earth was filled with a wonderful light between red sunset lingering over the mountain and that marvelous glory that shone into the woods from the summit of the hill. Darnell seemed to see some reflection of that wizard brightness in the room; the pale walls and the white bed and his wife's face lying amidst brown lair upon the pillow were illuminated, and listening he could almost hear the corncrake in the fields, the fern-owl sounding his strange note from the quiet of the rugged place where the bracken grew, and, like the echo of a magic song, the melody of the nightingale that sang all night in the alder by the little brook. There was nothing that he could say, but he slowly stole his arm under his wife's neck, and played with the ringlets of brown hair. She never moved, she lay there gently breathing, looking up to the blank ceiling of the room with her beautiful eyes, thinking also, no doubt, thoughts that she could not utter, kissing her husband obediently when he asked her to do so, and he stammered and hesitated as he spoke.

They were nearly asleep, indeed Darnell was on the very eve of dreaming, when she said very softly —

"I am afraid, darling, that we could never afford it." And he heard her words through the murmur of the water, dripping from the grey rock, and falling into the clear pool beneath.

Sunday morning was always an occasion of idleness. Indeed, they would never have got breakfast if Mrs. Darnell, who had the instincts of the housewife, had not awoke and seen the bright sunshine, and felt that the house was too still. She lay quiet for five minutes, while her husband slept beside her, and listened intently, waiting for the sound of Alice stirring down below. A golden tube of sunlight shone through some opening in the Venetian blinds, and it shone on the brown hair that lay about her head on the pillow, and she looked steadily into the room at the "duchesse" toilet-table, the colored ware of the washstand, and the two photogravures in oak frames, "The Meeting" and "The Parting," that hung upon the wall. She was half dreaming as she listened for the servant's footsteps, and the faint shadow of a shade of a thought came over her, and she imagined dimly, for the quick moment of a dream, another world where rapture was wine, where one wandered in a deep and happy valley, and the moon was always rising red above the trees. She was thinking of Hampstead, which represented to her the vision of the world beyond the walls, and the thought of the heath led her away to Bank Holidays, and then to Alice. There was not a sound in the house; it might have been midnight for the stillness if the drawling cry of the Sunday paper had not suddenly echoed round the corner of Edna Road, and with it came the warning clank and shriek of the milkman with his pails.

Mrs. Darnell sat up, and wide awake, listened more intently. The girl was evidently fast asleep, and must be roused, or all the work of the day would be out of joint, and she remembered how Edward hated any fuss or discussion about household matters, more especially on a Sunday, after his long week's work in the City. She gave her husband an affectionate glance as he slept on, for she was very fond of him, and so she gently rose from the bed and went in her nightgown to call the maid.

The servant's room was small and stuffy, the night had been very hot, and Mrs. Darnell paused for a moment at the door, wondering whether the girl on the bed was really the dusty-faced servant who bustled day by day about the house, or even the strangely bedizened creature, dressed in purple, with a shiny face, who would appear on the Sunday afternoon, bringing in an early tea, because it was her "evening out." Alice's hair was black and her skin was pale, almost of the olive tinge, and she lay asleep, her head resting on one arm, reminding Mrs. Darnell of a queer print of a "Tired Bacchante" that she had seen long ago in a shop window in Upper Street, Islington. And a cracked bell was ringing; that meant five minutes to eight, and nothing done.

She touched the girl gently on the shoulder, and only smiled when her eyes opened, and waking with a start, she got up in sudden confusion. Mrs. Darnell went back to her room and dressed slowly while her husband still slept, and it was only at the last moment, as she fastened her cherry-colored bodice, that she roused him, telling him that the bacon would be overdone unless he hurried over his dressing.

Over the breakfast they discussed the question of the spare room all over again. Mrs. Darnell still admitted that the plan of furnishing it attracted her, but she could not see how it could be done for the ten pounds, and as they were prudent people they did not care to encroach on their swings. Edward was highly paid, having (with allowances for extra work in busy weeks) a hundred and forty pounds a year, and Mary had inherited from an old uncle, her godfather, three hundred pounds, which had been judiciously laid out in mortgage at 4½ percent. Their total income, then, counting in Aunt Marian's present, was a hundred and fifty-eight pounds a year and they were clear of debt, since Darnell had bought the furniture for the house out of money which he had saved for five or six years before. In the first few years of his life in the City his income had, of course, been smaller, and at first he had lived very freely, without a thought of laying by. The theaters and music halls had attracted him, and scarcely a week passed without his going (in the pit) to one or the other; and he had occasionally bought photographs of actresses who pleased him. These he had solemnly burned when he became engaged to Mary; he remembered the evening well; his heart had been so full of joy and wonder, and the landlady had complained bitterly of the mess in the grate when he came home from the City the next night. Still, the money was lost, as far as he could recollect, ten or twelve shillings; and it annoyed him all the more to reflect that if he had put it by, it would have gone far toward the purchase of an "Orient" carpet in brilliant colors. Then there had been other expenses of his youth: he had purchased threepenny and even fourpenny cigars, the latter rarely, but the former frequently, sometimes singly, and sometimes in bundles of twelve for half-a-crown. Once a meerschaum pipe had haunted him for six weeks; the tobacconist had drawn it out of a drawer with some air of secrecy as he was buying a packet of "Lone Star." Here was another useless expense, these American-manufactured tobaccos; his "Lone Star," "Long Judge," "Old Hank," "Sultry Clime," and the rest of them cost from a shilling to one and six the two-ounce packet; whereas now he got excellent loose honeydew for threepence halfpenny an ounce. But the crafty tradesman, who had marked him down as a buyer of expensive fancy goods, nodded with his air of mystery, and, snapping open the case, displayed the meerschaum before the dazzled eyes of Darnell. The bowl was carved in the likeness of a female figure, showing the head and *torso,* and the mouthpiece was of the very best amber — only twelve and six, the man said, and the amber alone, he declared, was worth more than that. He explained that he felt some delicacy about showing the pipe to any but a regular customer, and was willing to take a little under cost price and "cut the loss." Darnell resisted for the time, but the pipe troubled him, and at last he bought it. He was pleased to show it to the younger men in the office for a while, but it never smoked very well, and he gave it away just before his marriage, as from the nature of the carving it would have been impossible to use it in his wife's presence. Once, while he was taking his holidays at Hastings, he had purchased a Malacca cane — a useless thing that had cost seven shillings — and he reflected with sorrow on the innumerable evenings on which he had rejected his landlady's plain fried chop, and had gone out to *flaner* among the Italian restaurants in Upper Street, Islington (he lodged in Holloway), pampering himself with expensive delicacies: cutlets and green peas, braised beef with tomato sauce, fillet steak and chipped potatoes, ending the banquet very often with a small wedge of Gruyère, which cost twopence. One night, after receiving a rise in his salary, he had actually drunk a quarter-flask of Chianti and had added the enormities of Benedictine, coffee, and

cigarettes to an expenditure already disgraceful, and
sixpence to the waiter made the bill amount to four
shillings instead of the shilling that would have pro-
vided him with a wholesome and sufficient repast at
home. Oh, there were many other items in this account
of extravagance, and Darnell had often regretted his
way of life, thinking that if he had been more careful,
five or six pounds a year might have been added to
their income.

And the question of the spare room brought back
these regrets in an exaggerated degree. He persuaded
himself that the extra five pounds would have given a
sufficient margin for the outlay that he desired to
make; though this was, no doubt, a mistake on his part.
But he saw quite clearly that, under the present condi-
tions, there must be no levies made on the very small
sum of money that they had saved. The rent of the
house was thirty-five, and rates and taxes added another ten pounds — nearly a quarter of their income
for houseroom. Mary kept down the housekeeping
bills to the very best of her ability, but meat was always
dear, and she suspected the maid of cutting surrepti-
tious slices from the joint and eating them in her
bedroom with bread and treacle in the dead of night,
for the girl had disordered and eccentric appetites. Mr.
Darnell thought no more of restaurants, cheap or dear;
he took his lunch with him to the City, and joined his
wife in the evening at high tea — chops, a bit of steak,
or cold meat from the Sunday's dinner. Mrs. Darnell
ate bread and jam and drank a little milk in the middle
of the day; but, with the utmost economy, the effort
to live within their means and to save for future con-
tingencies was a very hard one. They had determined
to do without change of air for at least three years, as
the honeymoon at Walton-on-the-Naze had cost a good
deal; and it was on this ground that they had, somewhat

illogically, reserved the ten pounds, declaring that as they were not to have any holiday they would spend the money on something useful.

And it was this consideration of utility that was finally fatal to Darnell's scheme. They had calculated and recalculated the expense of the bed and bedding, the linoleum, and the ornaments, and by a great deal of exertion the total expenditure had been made to assume the shape of "something very little over ten pounds," when Mary said quite suddenly — "But, after all, Edward, we don't really *want* to furnish the room at all. I mean it isn't necessary. And if we did so it might lead to no end of expense. People would hear of it and be sure to fish for invitations. You know we have relatives in the country, and they would be almost certain, the Mallings, at any rate, to give hints."

Darnell saw the force of the argument and gave way. But he was bitterly disappointed.

"It would have been very nice, wouldn't it?" he said with a sigh.

"Never mind, dear," said Mary, who saw that he was a good deal cast down. "We must think of some other plan that will be nice and useful too."

She often spoke to him in that tone of a kind mother, though she was by three years the younger.

"And now," she said, "I must get ready for church. Are you coming?"

Darnell said that he thought not. He usually accompanied his wife to morning service, but that day he felt some bitterness in his heart, and preferred to lounge under the shade of the big mulberry tree that stood in the middle of their patch of garden — relic of the spacious lawns that had once lain smooth and green and sweet, where the dismal streets now swarmed in a hopeless labyrinth.

So Mary went quietly and alone to church. St. Paul's

stood in a neighboring street, and its Gothic design
would have interested a curious inquirer into the history of a strange revival. Obviously, mechanically,
there was nothing amiss. The style chosen was "geo-
metrical decorated," and the tracery of the windows
seemed correct. The nave, the aisles, the spacious chancel, were reasonably proportioned; and, to be quite
serious, the only feature obviously wrong was the sub-
stitution of a low "chancel wall" with iron gates for
the rood screen with the loft and rood. But this, it
might plausibly be contended, was merely an adapta-
tion of the old idea to modern requirements, and it
would have been quite difficult to explain why the
whole building, from the mere mortar setting between
the stones to the Gothic gas standards, was a mysterious and elaborate blasphemy. The canticles were sung
to Joll in B flat, the chants were "Anglican," and the
sermon was the gospel for the day, amplified and
rendered into the more modern and graceful English
of the preacher. And Mary came away.

After their dinner (an excellent piece of Australian
mutton, bought in the "World Wide" Stores, in Hammersmith), they sat for some time in the garden, partly
sheltered by the big mulberry tree from the observation
of their neighbors. Edward smoked his honeydew, and
Mary looked at him with placid affection.

"You never tell me about the men in your office,"
she said at length. "Some of them are nice fellows,
aren't they?"

"Oh, yes, they're very decent. I must bring some of
them round, one of these days." He remembered with
a pang that it would be necessary to provide whisky.
One couldn't ask the guest to drink table beer at
tenpence the gallon.

"Who are they, though?" said Mary. "I think they
might have given you a wedding present."

"Well, I don't know. We never have gone in for that sort of thing. But they're very decent chaps. Well, there's Harvey; 'Sauce' they call him behind his back. He's mad on bicycling. He went in last year for the Two Miles Amateur Record. He'd have made it, too, if he could have got into better training.

"Then there's James, a sporting man. You wouldn't care for him. I always think he smells of the stable."

"How horrid!" said Mrs. Darnell, finding her husband a little frank, lowering her eyes as she spoke.

"Dickenson might amuse you," Darnell went on. "He's always got a joke. A terrible liar, though. When he tells a tale we never know how much to believe. He swore the other day he'd seen one of the governors buying cockles off a barrow near London Bridge, and Jones, who's just come, believed every word of it."

Darnell laughed at the humorous recollection of the jest.

"And that wasn't a bad yarn about Salter's wife," he went on. "Salter is the manager, you know. Dickenson lives close by, in Notting Hill, and he said one morning that he had seen Mrs. Salter, in the Portobello Road, in red stockings, dancing to a piano organ."

"He's a little coarse, isn't he?" said Mrs. Darnell. "I don't see much fun in that."

"Well, you know, amongst men it s different. You might like Wallis; he's a tremendous photographer. He often shows us photos he's taken of his children — one, a little girl of three, in her bath. I asked him how he thought she'd like it when she was twenty-three."

Mrs. Darnell looked down and made no answer.

There was silence for some minutes while Darnell smoked his pipe. "I say, Mary," he said at length, "what do you say to our taking a paying guest?"

"A paying guest! I never thought of it. Where should we put him?"

"Why, I was thinking of the spare room. The plan would obviate your objection, wouldn't it? Lots of men in the City take them, and make money of it too. I dare say it would add ten pounds a year to our income. Redgrave, the cashier, finds it worth his while to take a large house on purpose. They have a regular lawn for tennis and a billiard-room."

Mary considered gravely, always with the dream in her eyes. "I don't think we could manage it, Edward," she said; "it would be inconvenient in many ways. She hesitated for a moment. "And I don't think I should care to have a young man in the house. It is so very small, and our accommodation, as you know, is so limited."

She blushed slightly, and Edward, a little disappointed as he was, looked at her with a singular longing, as if he were a scholar confronted with a doubtful hieroglyph, either wholly wonderful or altogether commonplace. Next door children were playing in the garden, playing shrilly, laughing crying, quarreling, racing to and fro. Suddenly a dear, pleasant voice sounded from an upper window.

"Enid! Charles! Come up to my room at once!"

There was an instant sudden hush. The children's voices died away.

"Mrs. Parker is supposed to keep her children in great order," said Mary. "Alice was telling me about it the other day. She had been talking to Mrs. Parker's servant. I listened to her without any remark, as I don't think it right to encourage servants' gossip; they always exaggerate everything. And I dare say children often require to be corrected."

The children were struck silent as if some ghastly terror had seized them.

Darnell fancied that he heard a queer sort of cry from the house, but could not be quite sure. He turned to the other side, where an elderly, ordinary man with a grey moustache was strolling up and down on the further side of his garden. He caught Darnell's eye, and Mrs. Darnell looking toward him at the same moment, he very politely raised his tweed cap. Darnell was surprised to see his wife blushing fiercely.

"Sayce and I often go into the City by the same 'bus," he said, "and as it happens we've sat next to each other two or three times lately. I believe he's a traveler for a leather firm in Bermondsey. He struck me as a pleasant man. Haven't they got rather a good-looking servant?"

"Alice has spoken to me about her — and the Sayces," said Mrs. Darnell. "I understand that they are not very well thought of in the neighborhood. But I must go in and see whether the tea is ready. Alice will be wanting to go out directly."

Darnell looked after his wife as she walked quickly away. He only dimly understood, but he could see the charm of her figure, the delight of the brown curls clustering about her neck, and he again felt that sense of the scholar confronted by the hieroglyphic. He could not have expressed his emotion, but he wondered whether he would ever find the key, and something told him that before she could speak to him his own lips must be unclosed. She had gone into the house by the back kitchen door, leaving it open, and he heard her speaking to the girl about the water being "really boiling." He was amazed, almost indignant with himself; but the sound of the words came to his ears as strange, heart-piercing music, tones from another, wonderful sphere. And yet he was her husband, and they had been married nearly a year; and yet, whenever she spoke, he had to listen to the sense of what she said, constraining himself, lest he should believe she was a magic creature, knowing the secrets of immeasurable delight.

He looked out through the leaves of the mulberry tree. Mr. Sayce had disappeared from his view, but he saw the light-blue fume of the cigar that he was smoking floating slowly across the shadowed air. He was wondering at his wife's manner when Sayce's name was mentioned, puzzling his head as to what could be amiss in the household of a most respectable personage, when his wife appeared at the dining room window and called him in to tea. She smiled as he looked up, and he rose hastily and walked in, wondering whether he were not a little "queer," so strange were the dim emotions and the dimmer impulses that rose within him.

Alice was all shining purple and strong scent, as she brought in the teapot and the jug of hot water. It seemed that a visit to the kitchen had inspired Mrs. Darnell in her turn with a novel plan for disposing of the famous ten pounds. The range had always been a trouble to her, and when sometimes she went into the kitchen, and found, as she said, the fire "roaring half-way up the chimney," it was in vain that she reproved the maid on the ground of extravagance and waste of coal. Alice was ready to admit the absurdity of making up such an enormous fire merely to bake (they called it "roast") a bit of beef or mutton, and to boil the potatoes and the cabbage; but she was able to show Mrs. Darnell that the fault lay in the defective contrivance of the range, in an oven which "would not get hot." Even with a chop or a steak it was almost as bad; the heat seemed to escape up the chimney or into the room, and Mary had spoken several times to her husband on the shocking waste of coal, and the cheapest coal procurable was never less than eighteen shillings the ton. Mr. Darnell had written to the landlord, a builder, who had replied in an illiterate but offensive communication, maintaining the excellence of the stove and charging all the faults to the account of "your good lady," which really implied that the Darnells kept no servant, and that Mrs. Darnell did everything. The range, then, remained, a standing annoyance and expense. Every morning, Alice said, she had the greatest difficulty in getting the fire to light at all, and once lighted it "seemed as if it fled right up the chimney." Only a few nights before Mrs. Darnell had spoken seriously to her husband about it; she had got Alice to weigh the coals expended in cooking a cottage pie, the dish of the evening, and deducting what remained in the scuttle after the pie was done, it appeared that the wretched thing had consumed nearly twice the proper quantity of fuel.

"You remember what I said the other night about the range?" said Mrs. Darnell, as she poured out the tea and watered the leaves. She thought the introduction a good one, for though her husband was a most amiable man, she guessed that he had been just a little hurt by her decision against his furnishing scheme.

"The range?" said Darnell. He paused as he helped himself to the marmalade and considered for a moment. "No, I don't recollect. What night was it?"

"Tuesday. Don't you remember? You had 'overtime,' and didn't get home till quite late." She paused for a moment, blushing slightly; and then began to recapitulate the misdeeds of the range, and the outrageous outlay of coal in the preparation of the cottage pie.

"Oh, I recollect now. That was the night I thought I heard the nightingale (people say there are nightingales in Bedford Park), and the sky was such a wonderful deep blue."

He remembered how he had walked from Uxbridge Road Station, where the green 'bus stopped, and in spite of the fuming kilns under Acton, a delicate odor of the woods and summer fields was mysteriously in

the air, and he had fancied that he smelt the red wild
roses, drooping from the hedge. As he came to his gate
he saw his wife standing in the doorway, with a light
in her hand, and he threw his arms violently about her
as she welcomed him, and whispered something in her
ear, kissing her scented hair. He had felt quite abashed
a moment afterward, and he was afraid that he had
frightened her by his nonsense; she seemed trembling
and confused. And then she had told him how they
had weighed the coal.

"Yes, I remember now," he said. "It is a great nuisance, isn't it? I hate to throw away money like that."

"Well, what do you think? Suppose we bought a
really good range with aunt's money? It would save us
a lot, and I expect the things would taste much nicer."

Darnell passed the marmalade, and confessed that
the idea was brilliant.

"It's much better than mine, Mary," he said quite
frankly. "I am so glad you thought of it. But we must
talk it over; it doesn't do to buy in a hurry. There are
so many makes."

Each had seen ranges which looked miraculous in-
ventions; he in the neighborhood of the City; she in
Oxford Street and Regent Street, on visits to the den-
tist. They discussed the matter at tea, and afterward
they discussed it walking round and round the garden,
in the sweet cool of the evening.

"They say the 'Newcastle' will burn anything, coke
even," said Mary.

"But the 'Glow' got the gold medal at the Paris
Exhibition," said Edward.

"But what about the 'Eutopia' Kitchener? Have you
seen it at work in Oxford Street?" said Mary. "They say
their plan of ventilating the oven is quite unique."

"I was in Fleet Street the other day," answered Edward, "and I was looking at the 'Bliss' Patent Stoves.

They burn less fuel than any in the market — so the makers declare."

He put his arm gently round her waist. She did not repel him; she whispered quite softly — "I think Mrs. Parker is at her window," and he drew his arm back slowly.

"But we will talk it over," he said. "There is no hurry. I might call at some of the places near the City, and you might do the same thing in Oxford Street and Regent Street and Piccadilly, and we could compare notes."

Mary was quite pleased with her husband's good temper. It was so nice of him not to find fault with her plan; "He's so good to me," she thought, and that was what she often said to her brother, who did not care much for Darnell. They sat down on the seat under the mulberry, close together, and she let Darnell take her hand, and as she felt his shy, hesitating fingers touch her in the shadow, she pressed them ever so softly, and as he fondled her hand, his breath was on her neck, and she heard his passionate, hesitating voice whisper, "My dear, my dear," as his lips touched her cheek. She trembled a little, and waited. Darnell kissed her gently on the cheek and drew away his band, and when he spoke he was almost breathless.

"We had better go in now," he said. "There is a heavy dew, and you might catch cold."

A warm, scented gale came to them from beyond the walls. He longed to ask her to stay out with him all night beneath the tree, that they might whisper to one another, that the scent of her hair might inebriate him, that he might feel her dress still brushing against his ankles. But he could not find the words, and it was absurd, and she was so gentle that she would do whatever he asked, however foolish it might be, just because he asked her. He was not worthy to kiss her lips; he bent down and kissed her silk bodice, and again he felt that she trembled, and he was ashamed, fearing that he had frightened her.

They went slowly into the house, side by side, and Darnell lit the gas in the drawing room, where they always sat on Sunday evenings. Mrs. Darnell felt a little tired and lay down on the sofa, and Darnell took the armchair opposite. For a while they were silent, and then Darnell said suddenly — "What's wrong with the Sayces? You seemed to think there was something a little strange about them. Their maid looks quite quiet."

"Oh, I don't know that one ought to pay any attention to servants' gossip. They're not always very truthful."

"It was Alice told you, wasn't it?"

"Yes. She was speaking to me the other day, when I was in the kitchen in the afternoon."

"But what was it?"

"Oh, I'd rather not tell you, Edward. It's not pleasant. I scolded Alice for repeating it to me." Darnell got up and took a small, frail chair near the sofa.

"Tell me," he said again, with an odd perversity. He did not really care to hear about the household next door, but he remembered how his wife's cheeks flushed in the afternoon, and now he was looking at her eyes.

"Oh, I really couldn't tell you, dear. I should feel ashamed."

"But you're my wife."

"Yes, but it doesn't make any difference. A woman doesn't like to talk about such things." Darnell bent his head down. His heart was beating; he put his ear to her mouth and said, "Whisper."

Mary drew his head down still lower with her gentle hand, and her cheeks burned as she whispered — "Alice says that — upstairs — they have only — one room furnished. The maid told her — herself." With an unconscious gesture she pressed his head to her breast, and he in turn was bending her red lips to his own, when a violent jangle clamored through the silent house. They sat up, and Mrs. Darnell went hurriedly to the door.

"That's Alice," she said. "She is always in in time. It has only just struck ten."

Darnell shivered with annoyance. His lips, he knew, had almost been opened. Mary's pretty handkerchief, delicately scented from a little flagon that a school friend had given her, lay on the floor, and he picked it up, and kissed it, and hid it away.

The question of the range occupied them all through June and far into July. Mrs. Darnell took every opportunity of going to the West End and investigating the capacity of the latest makes, gravely viewing the new improvements and hearing what the shopmen had to say; while Darnell, as he said, "kept his eyes open" about the City. They accumulated quite a literature of the subject, bringing away illustrated pamphlets, and in the evenings it was an amusement to look at the pictures. They viewed with reverence and interest the drawings of great ranges for hotels and public institutions, mighty contrivances furnished with a series of ovens each for a different use, with wonderful apparatus for grilling, with batteries of accessories which seemed to invest the cook almost with the dignity of a chief engineer. But when, in one of the lists, they encountered the images of little toy "cottage" ranges, for four pounds, and even for three pounds ten, they grew scornful, on the strength of the eight or ten pound article which they meant to purchase — when the merits of the divers patents had been thoroughly thrashed out.

The "Raven" was for a long time Mary's favorite. It

promised the utmost economy with the highest effi-
ciency, and many times they were on the point of
giving the order. But the "Glow" seemed equally seduc-
tive, and it was only £8. 5s. as compared with £9. 7s.
6d., and though the "Raven" was supplied to the Royal
Kitchen, the "Glow" could show more fervent testimo-
nials from continental potentates.

It seemed a debate without end, and it endured day
after day till that morning, when Darnell woke from
the dream of the ancient wood, of the fountains rising
into grey vapor beneath the heat of the sun. As he
dressed, an idea struck him, and he brought it as a
shock to the hurried breakfast, disturbed by the
thought of the City 'bus which passed the corner of
the street at 9:15. "I've got an improvement on your
plan, Mary," he said, with triumph. "Look at that,"
and he flung a little book on the table.

He laughed. "It beats your notion all to fits. After
all, the great expense is the coal. It's not the stove — at
least that's not the real mischief. It's the coal is so dear.
And here you are. Look at those oil stoves. They don't
burn any coal, but the cheapest fuel in the world — oil;
and for two pounds ten you can get a range that will
do everything you want."

"Give me the book," said Mary, "and we will talk it
over in the evening, when you come home. Must you
be going?"

Darnell cast an anxious glance at the clock.

"Good-bye," and they kissed each other seriously
and dutifully, and Mary's eyes made Darnell think of
those lonely water-pools, hidden in the shadow of the
ancient goods.

So, day after day, he lived in the grey phantasmal
world, akin to death, that has, somehow, with most of
us, made good its claim to be called life. To Darnell
the true life would have seemed madness, and when,

now and again, the shadows and vague images reflected from its splendor fell across his path, he was afraid, and took refuge in what he would have called the sane "reality" of common and usual incidents and interests. His absurdity was, perhaps, the more evident, inasmuch as "reality" for him was a matter of kitchen ranges, of saving a few shillings; but in truth the folly would have been greater if it had been concerned with racing stables, steam yachts, and the spending of many thousand pounds.

But so went forth Darnell, day by day, strangely mistaking death for life, madness for sanity, and purposeless and wandering phantoms for true beings. He was sincerely of opinion that he was a City clerk, living in Shepherd's Bush — having forgotten the mysteries and the far-shining glories of the kingdom which was his by legitimate inheritance.

II

All day long a fierce and heavy heat had brooded Over the City, and as Darnel neared home he saw the mist lying on all the damp lowlands, wreathed in coils about Bedford Park to the south, and mounting to the West, so that the tower of Acton Church loomed out of a grey lake. The grass in the squares and on the lawns which he overlooked as the 'bus lumbered wearily along was burned to the color of dust. Shepherd's Bush Green was a wretched desert, trampled brown, bordered with monotonous poplars, whose leaves hung motionless in air that was still, hot smoke. The foot passengers struggled wearily along the pavements, and the reek of the summer's end mingled with the breath of the brickfields made

Darnell gasp, as if he were inhaling the poison of some foul sick-room.

He made but a slight inroad into the cold mutton that adorned the tea-table, and confessed that he felt rather "done up" by the weather and the day's work.

"I have had a trying day, too," said Mary. "Alice has been very queer and troublesome all day, and I have had to speak to her quite seriously. You know I think her Sunday evenings out have a rather unsettling influence on the girl. But what is one to do?"

"Has she got a young man?"

"Of course: a grocer's assistant from the Goldhawk Road — Wilkin's, you know. I tried them when we settled here, but they were not very satisfactory."

"What do they do with themselves all the evening? They have from five to ten, haven't they?"

"Yes; five, or sometimes half-past, when the water won't boil. Well, I believe they go for walks usually. Once or twice he has taken her to the City Temple, and the Sunday before last they walked up and down Oxford Street, and then sat in the Park. But it seems that last Sunday they went to tea with his mother at Putney. I should like to tell the old woman what I really think of her."

"Why? What happened? Was she nasty to the girl?"

"No; that's just it. Before this, she has been very unpleasant on several occasions. When the young man first took Alice to see her — that was in March — the girl came away crying; she told me so herself. Indeed, she said she never wanted to see old Mrs. Murry again; and I told Alice that, if she had not exaggerated things, I could hardly blame her for feeling like that."

"Why? What did she cry for?"

"Well, it seems that the old lady — she lives in quite a small cottage in some Putney back street — was so stately that she would hardly speak. She had borrowed a little girl from some neighbor's family, and had managed to dress her up to imitate a servant, and Alice said nothing could be sillier than to see that mite opening the door, with her black dress and her white cap and apron, and she hardly able to turn the handle, as Alice said. George (that's the young man's name) had told Alice that it was a little bit of a house; but he said the kitchen was comfortable, though very plain and old-fashioned. But, instead of going straight to the back, and sitting by a big fire on the old settle that they had brought up from the country, that child asked for their names (did you ever hear such nonsense?) and showed them into a little poky parlor, where old Mrs. Murry was sitting 'like a duchess,' by a fireplace full of colored paper, and the room as cold as ice. And she was so grand that she would hardly speak to Alice."

"That must have been very unpleasant."

"Oh, the poor girl had a dreadful time. She began with: 'Very pleased to make your acquaintance, Miss Dill. I know so very few persons in service.' Alice imitates her mincing way of talking, but I can't do it. And then she went on to talk about her family, how they had farmed their own land for five hundred years — such stuff! George had told Alice all about it: they had had an old cottage with a good strip of garden and two fields somewhere in Essex, and that old woman talked almost as if they had been country gentry, and boasted about the Rector, Dr. Somebody, coming to see them so often, and of Squire Somebody Else always looking them up, as if they didn't visit them out of kindness. Alice told me it was as much as she could do to keep from laughing in Mrs. Murry's face, her young man having told her all about the place, and how small it was, and how the Squire had been so kind about buying it when old Murry died and George was a little boy, and his mother not able to keep things going.

However, that silly old woman 'laid it on thick,' as you say, and the young man got more and more uncomfortable, especially when she went on to speak about marrying in one's own class, and how unhappy she had known young men to be who had married beneath them, giving some very pointed looks at Alice as she talked. And then such an amusing thing happened: Alice had noticed George looking about him in a puzzled sort of way, as if he couldn't make out something or other, and at last he burst out and asked his mother if she had been buying up the neighbors' ornaments, as he remembered the two green cut-glass vases on the mantelpiece at Mrs. Ellis's, and the wax flowers at Miss Turvey's. He was going on, but his mother scowled at him, and upset some books, which he had to pick up; but Alice quite understood she had been borrowing things from her neighbors, just as she had borrowed the little girl, so as to look grander. And then they had tea — water bewitched, Alice calls it — and very thin bread and butter, and rubbishy foreign pastry from the Swiss shop in the High Street — all sour froth and rancid fat, Alice declares. And then Mrs. Murry began boasting again about her family, and snubbing Alice and talking at her, till the girl came away quite furious, and very unhappy, too. I don't wonder at it, do you?"

"It doesn't sound very enjoyable, certainly," said Darnell, looking dreamily at his wife. He had not been attending very carefully to the subject-matter of her story, but he loved to hear a voice that was incantation in his ears, tones that summoned before him the vision of a magic world.

"And has the young man's mother always been like this?" he said after a long pause, desiring that the musk should continue.

"Always, till quite lately, till last Sunday in fact. Of

course Alice spoke to George Murry at once, and said,
like a sensible girl, that she didn't think it ever answered for a married couple to live with the man's
mother, 'especially,' she went on, 'as I can see your
mother hasn't taken much of a fancy to me.' He told
her, in the usual style, it was only his mother's way,
that she didn't really mean anything, and so on; but
Alice kept away for a long time, and rather hinted, I
think, that it might come to having to choose between
her and his mother. And so affairs went on all through
the spring and summer, and then, just before the
August Bank Holiday, George spoke to Alice again
about it, and told her how sorry the thought of any
unpleasantness made him, and how he wanted his
mother and her to get on with each other, and how
she was only a bit old-fashioned and queer in her ways,
and had spoken very nicely to him about her when
there was nobody by. So the long and the short of it
was that Alice said she might come with them on the
Monday, when they had settled to go to Hampton
Court – the girl was always talking about Hampton
Court, and wanting to see it. You remember what a
beautiful day it was, don't you?"

"Let me see," said Darnell dreamily. "Oh yes, of
course – I sat out under the mulberry tree all day, and
we had our meals there: it was quite a picnic. The
caterpillars were a nuisance, but I enjoyed the day very
much." His ears were charmed, ravished with the grave,
supernal melody, as of antique song, rather of the first
made world in which all speech was descant, and all
words were sacraments of might, speaking not to the
mind but to the soul. He lay back in his chair, and said
– "Well, what happened to them?"

"My dear, would you believe it; but that wretched
old woman behaved worse than ever. They met as had
been arranged, at Kew Bridge, and got places, with a

good deal of difficulty, in one of those charàbanc things, and Alice thought she was going to enjoy herself tremendously. Nothing of the kind. They had hardly said 'Good morning,' when old Mrs. Murry began to talk about Kew Gardens, and how beautiful it must be there, and how much more convenient it was than Hampton, and no expense at all; just the trouble of walking over the bridge. Then she went on to say, as they were waiting for the charàbanc, that she had always heard there was nothing to see at Hampton, except a lot of nasty, grimy old pictures, and some of them not fit for any decent woman, let alone girl, to look at, and she wondered why the Queen allowed such things to be shown, putting all kinds of notions into girls' heads that were light enough already; and as she said that she looked at Alice so nastily — horrid old thing — that, as she told me afterward, Alice would have slapped her face if she hadn't been an elderly woman, and George's mother. Then she talked about Kew again, saying how wonderful the hothouses were, with palms and all sorts of wonderful things, and a lily as big as a parlor table, and the view over the river. George was very good, Alice told me. He was quite taken aback at first, as the old woman had promised faithfully to be as nice as ever she could be; but then he said, gently but firmly, 'Well, mother, we must go to Kew some other day, as Alice has set her heart on Hampton for today, and I want to see it myself!' All Mrs. Murry did was to snort, and look at the girl like vinegar, and just then the char-a-bane came up, and they had to scramble for their seats. Mrs. Mummy grumbled to herself in an indistinct sort of voice all the way to Hampton Court. Alice couldn't very well make out what she said, but now and then she seemed to hear bits of sentences, like: *Pity to grow old, if Sons grow bold;* and *Honor thy father and mother;* and *Lie on the shelf, said the housewife to the old shoe, and the wicked son to his mother;* and *I gave you milk and you give me the go-by.* Alice thought they must be proverbs (except the Commandment, of course), as George was always saying how old-fashioned his mother is; but she says there were so many of them, and all pointed at her and George, that she thinks now Mrs. Murry must have made them up as they drove along. She says it would be just like her to do it, being old-fashioned, and ill-natured too, and fuller of talk than a butcher on Saturday night. Well, they got to Hampton at last, and Alice thought the place would please her, perhaps, and they might have some enjoyment. But she did nothing but grumble, and out loud too, so that people looked at them, and a woman said, so that they could hear, 'Ah well, they'll be old themselves some day,' which made Alice very angry, for, as she said, they weren't doing anything. When they showed her the chestnut avenue in Bushey Park, she said it was so long and straight that it made her quite dull to look at it, and she thought the deer (you know how pretty they are, really) looked thin and miserable, as if they would be all the better for a good feed of hog-wash, with plenty of meal in it. She said she knew they weren't happy by the look in their eyes, which seemed to tell hem that their keepers beat them. It was the same with everything; she said she remembered market-gardens in Hammersmith and Gunnersbury that had a better show of flowers, and when they took her to the place where the water is, under the trees, she burst out with its being rather hard to tramp her off her legs to show her a common canal, with not so much as a barge on it to liven it up a bit. She went on like that the whole day, and Alice told me she was only too thankful to get home and get rid of her. Wasn't it wretched for the girl?"

"It must have been, indeed. But what happened last Sunday?"

"That's the most extraordinary thing of all. I noticed that Alice was rather queer in her manner this morning; she was a longer time washing up the breakfast things, and she answered me quite sharply when I called to her to ask when she would be ready to help me with the wash; and when I went into the kitchen to see about something, I noticed that she was going about her work in a sulky sort of way. So I asked her what was the matter, and then it all came out. I could scarcely believe my own ears when she mumbled out something about Mrs. Murry thinking she could do very much better for herself; but I asked her one question after another till I had it all out of her. It just shows one how foolish and empty-headed these girls are. I told her she was no better than a weather-cock. If you will believe me, that horrid old woman was quite another person when Alice went to see her the other night. Why, I can't think, but so she was. She told the girl how pretty she was; what a neat figure she had; how well she walked; and how she'd known many a girl not half so clever or well-looking earning her twenty-five or thirty pounds a year, and with good families. She seems to have gone into all sorts of details, and made elaborate calculations as to what she would be able to save, 'with decent folks, who don't screw, and pinch, and lock up everything in the house,' and then she went off into a lot of hypocritical nonsense about how fond she was of Alice, and how she could go to her grave in peace, knowing how happy her dear George would be with such a good wife, and about her savings from good wages helping to set up a little home, ending up with 'And, if you take an old woman's advice, deary, it won't be long before you hear the marriage bells.'

"I see," said Darnell; "and the upshot of it all is, I

suppose, that the girl is thoroughly dissatisfied?"

"Yes, she is so young and silly. I talked to her, and reminded her of how nasty old Mrs. Murry had been, and told her that she might change her place and change for the worse. I think I have persuaded her to think it over quietly, at all events. Do you know what it is, Edward? I have an idea. I believe that wicked old woman is trying to get Alice to leave us, that she may tell her son how changeable she is; and I suppose she would make up some of her stupid old proverbs: 'A changeable wife, a troublesome life,' or some nonsense of the kind. Horrid old thing!"

"Well, well," said Darnell, "I hope she won't go, for your sake. It would be such a bother for you, hunting for a fresh servant."

He refilled his pipe and smoked placidly, refreshed somewhat after the emptiness and the burden of the day. The French window was wide open, and now at last there came a breath of quickening air, distilled by the night from such trees as still wore green in that arid valley. The song to which Darnell had listened in rapture, and now the breeze, which even in that dry, grim suburb still bore the word of the woodland, had summoned the dream to his eyes, and he meditated over matters that his lips could not express.

"She must, indeed, be a villainous old woman," he said at length.

"Old Mrs. Murry? Of course she is; the mischievous old thing! Trying to take the girl from a comfortable place where she is happy."

"Yes; and not to like Hampton Court! That shows bow bad she must be, more than anything."

"It is beautiful, isn't it?"

"I shall never forget the first time I saw it. It was soon after I went into the City; the first year. I had my holidays in July, and I was getting such a small salary that I couldn't think of going away to the seaside, or anything like that. I remember one of the other men wanted me to come with him on a walking tour in Kent. I should have liked that, but the money wouldn't run to it. And do you know what I did? I lived in Great College Street then, and the first day I was off, I stayed in bed till past dinner-time, and lounged about in an armchair with a pipe all the afternoon. I had got a new kind of tobacco — one and four for the two-ounce packet — much dearer than I could afford to smoke, and I was enjoying it immensely. It was awfully hot, and when I shut the window and drew down the red blind it grew hotter; at five o'clock the room was like an oven. But I was so pleased at not having to go into the City, that I didn't mind anything, and now and again I read bits from a queer old book that had belonged to my poor dad. I couldn't make out what a lot of it meant, but it fitted in somehow, and I read and smoked till teatime. Then I went out for a walk, thinking I should be better for a little fresh air before I went to bed; and I went wandering away, not much noticing where I was going, turning here and theme as the fancy took me. I must have gone miles and miles, and a good many of them mound and round, as they say they do in Australia if they lose their way in the bush; and I am sure I couldn't have gone exactly the same way all over again for any money. Anyhow, I was still in the streets when the twilight came on, and the lamp-lighters were trotting round from one lamp to another. It was a wonderful night: I wish you had been theme, my dear."

"I was quite a little girl then."

"Yes, I suppose you were. Well, it was a wonderful night. I remember, I was walking in a little street of little grey houses all alike, with stucco copings and stucco doorposts; there were brass plates on a lot of the doors, and one had 'Maker of Shell Boxes' on it, and I was quite pleased, as I had often wondered where those boxes and things that you buy at the seaside came from. A few children were playing about in the road with some rubbish or other, and men were singing in a small public-house at the corner, and I happened to look up, and I noticed what a wonderful color the sky had turned. I have seen it since, but I don't think it has ever been quite what it was that night, a dark blue, glowing like a violet, just as they say the sky looks in foreign countries. I don't know why, but the sky or something made me feel quite queer; everything seemed changed in a way I couldn't understand. I remember, I told an old gentleman I knew then — a friend of my poor father's, he's been dead for five years, if not more — about how I felt, and he looked at me and said something about fairyland; I don't know what he meant, and I dare say I didn't explain myself properly. But, do you know, for a moment or two I felt as if that little back street was beautiful, and the noise of the children and the men in the public-house seemed to fit in with the sky and become part of it. You know that old saying about 'treading on air' when one is glad! Well, I really felt like that as I walked, not exactly like air, you know, but as if the pavement was velvet or some very soft carpet. And then — I suppose it was all my fancy — the air seemed to smell sweet, like the incense in Catholic churches, and my breath came queer and catchy, as it does when one gets very excited about anything. I felt altogether stranger than I've ever felt before or since."

Darnell stopped suddenly and looked up at his wife. She was watching him with parted lips, with eager, wondering eyes.

"I hope I'm not tiring you, dear, with all this story about nothing. You have had a worrying day with that stupid girl; hadn't you better go to bed?"

"Oh, no, please, Edward. I'm not a bit timed now. I love to hear you talk like that. Please go on."

"Well, after I had walked a bit further, that queer sort of feeling seemed to fade away. I said a bit further, and I really thought I had been walking about five minutes, but I had looked at my watch just before I got into that little street, and when I looked at it again it was eleven o'clock. I must have done about eight miles. I could scarcely believe my own eyes, and I thought my watch must have gone mad; but I found out afterward it was perfectly right. I couldn't make it out, and I can't now; I assure you the time passed as if I walked up one side of Edna Road and down the other. But there I was, right in the open country, with a cool wind blowing on me from a wood, and the air full of soft rustling sounds, and notes of birds from the bushes, and the singing noise of a little brook that ran under the road. I was standing on the bridge when I took out my watch and struck a wax light to see the time; and it came upon me suddenly what a strange evening it had been. It was all so different, you see, to what I had been doing all my life, particularly for the year before, and it almost seemed as if I couldn't be the man who had been going into the City every day in the morning and coming back from it every evening after writing a lot of uninteresting letters. It was like being pitched all of a sudden from one world into another. Well, I found my way back somehow or other, and as I went along I made up my mind how I'd spend my holiday. I said to myself, 'I'll have a walking tour as well as Ferrars, only mine is to be a tour of London and its environs,' and I had got it all settled when I let myself into the house about four o'clock in the morning, and the sun was shining, and the street almost as still as the wood at midnight!"

"I think that was a capital idea of yours. Did you have your tour? Did you buy a map of London?"

"I had the tour all right. I didn't buy a map; that would have spoilt it, somehow; to see everything plotted out, and named, and measured. What I wanted was to feel that I was going where nobody had been before. That's nonsense, isn't it? as if there could be any such places in London, or England either, for the matter of that."

"I know what you mean; you wanted to feel as if you were going on a sort of voyage of discovery. Isn't that it?"

"Exactly, that's what I was trying to tell you. Besides, I didn't want to buy a map. I made a map."

"How do you mean? Did you make a map out of your head?"

"I'll tell you about it afterward. But do you really want to hear" about my grand tour?"

"Of course I do; it must have been delightful. I call it a most original idea."

"Well, I was quite full of it, and what you said just now about a voyage of discovery reminds me of how I felt then. When I was a boy I was awfully fond of reading of great travelers — I suppose all boys are — and of sailors who were driven out of their tourse and found themselves in latitudes where no ship had ever sailed before, and of people. who discovered wonderful cities in strange countries; and all the second day of my holidays I was feeling just as I used to when I read these books. I didn't get up till pretty late. I was tired to death after all those miles I had walked; but when I had finished my breakfast and filled my pipe, I had a grand time of it. It was such nonsense, you know; as if there could be anything strange or wonderful in London."

"Why shouldn't there be?"

"Well, I don't know; but I have thought afterward what a silly lad I must have been. Anyhow, I had a great day of it, planning what I would do, half making-believe — just like a kid — that I didn't know where I might find myself, or what might happen to me. And I was enormously pleased to think it was all my secret, that nobody else knew anything about it, and that, whatever I might see, I would keep to myself. I had always felt like that about the books. Of course, I loved reading them, but it seemed to me that, if I had been a discoverer, I would have kept my discoveries a secret. If I had been Columbus, and, if it could possibly have been managed, I would have found America all by myself, and never have said a word about it to anybody. Fancy! how beautiful it would be to be walking about in one's own town, and talking to people, and all the while to have the thought that one knew of a great world beyond the seas, that nobody else dreamed of. I should have loved that!

"And that is exactly what I felt about the tour I was going to make. I made up my mind that nobody should know; and so, from that day to this, nobody has heard a word of it."

"But you are going to tell me?"

"You are different. Rut I don't think even you will hear everything; not because I won't, but because I can't tell many of the things I saw."

"Things you saw? Then you really did see wonderful, strange things in London?"

"Well, I did and I didn't. Everything, or pretty nearly everything, that I saw is standing still, and hundreds of thousands of people have looked at the same sights — there were many places that the fellows in the office knew quite well, I found out afterward. And then I read a book called 'London and its Surroundings.' But (I don't know how it is) neither the men at the office nor the writers of the book seem to have seen the things that I did. That's why I stopped reading the book; it seemed to take the life, the real heart, out of everything, making it as dry and stupid as the stuffed birds in a museum.

"I thought about what I was going to do all that day, and went to bed early, so as to be fresh. I knew wonderfully little about London, really; though, except for an odd week now and then, I had spent all my life in town. Of course I knew the main streets — the Strand, Regent Street, Oxford Street, and so on — and I knew the way to the school I used to go to when I was a boy, and the way into the City. But I had just kept to a few tracks, as they say the sheep do on the mountains; and that made it all the easier for me to imagine that I was going to discover a new world."

Darnell paused in the stream of his talk. He looked keenly at his wife to see if he were wearying her, but her eyes gazed at him with unabated interest — one would have almost said that they were the eyes of one who longed and half expected to be initiated into the mysteries, who knew not what great wonder was to be revealed. She sat with her back to the open window, framed in the sweet dusk of the night, as if a painter had made a curtain of heavy velvet behind her; and the work that she had been doing had fallen to the floor. She supported her head with her two hands placed on each side of her brow, and her eyes were as the wells in the wood of which Darnell dreamed in the night-time and in the day.

"And all the strange tales I had ever heard were in my head that morning," he went on, as if continuing the thoughts that had filled his mind while his lips were silent. "I had gone to bed early, as I told you, to get a thorough rest, and I had set my alarum clock to wake me at three, so that I might set out at an hour that was quite strange for the beginning of a journey. There was a hush in the world when I awoke, before the clock had rung to arouse me, and then a bird began to sing and twitter in the elm tree that grew in the next garden, and I looked out of the window, and everything was still, and the morning air breathed in pure and sweet, as I had never known it before. My room was at the back of the house, and most of the gardens had trees in them, and beyond these trees I could see the backs of the houses of the next street rising like the wall of an old city; and as I looked the sun rose, and the great light came in at my window, and the day began.

"And I found that when I was once out of the streets just about me that I knew, some of the queer feeling that had come to me two days before came back again. It was not nearly so strong, the streets no longer smelt of incense, but still there was enough of it to show me what a strange world I passed by. There were things that one may see again and again in many London streets: a vine or a fig tree on a wall, a lark singing in a cage, a curious shrub blossoming in a garden, an odd shape of a roof, or a balcony with an uncommon-looking trelliswork in iron. There's scarcely a street, perhaps, where you won't see one or other of such things as these; but that morning they rose to my eyes in a new light, as if I had on the magic spectacles in the fairy tale, and just like the man in the fairy tale, I went on and on in the new light. I remember going through wild land on a high place; there were pools of water shining in the sun, and great white houses in the middle of dark, rocking pines, and then on the turn of the height I came to a little lane that went aside from the main road, a lane that led to a wood, and in the lane was a little old shadowed house, with a bell turret in the roof, and a porch of trelliswork all dim and faded into the color of the sea; and in the garden there were growing tall, white lilies, just as we saw them that day we went to look at the old pictures; they were shining like silver, and they filled the air with their sweet scent. It was from near that house I saw the valley and high places far away in the sun. So, as I say, I went 'on and on,' by woods and fields, till I came to a little town on the top of a hill, a town full of old houses bowing to the ground beneath their years, and the morning was so still that the blue smoke rose up straight into the sky from all the roof-tops, so still that I heard far down in the valley the song of a boy who was singing an old song through the streets as he went to school, and as I passed through the awakening town, beneath the old, grave houses, the church bells began to ring.

"It was soon after I had left this town behind me that I found the Strange Road. I saw it branching off from the dusty high road, and it looked so green that I turned aside into it, and soon I felt as if I had really come into a new country. I don't know whether it was one of the roads the old Romans made that my father used to tell me about; but it was covered with deep, soft turf, and the great tall hedges on each side looked as if they had not been touched for a hundred years; they had grown so broad and high and wild that they met overhead, and I could only get glimpses here and there of the country through which I was passing, as one passes in a dream. The Strange Road led me on and on, up and down hill; sometimes the rose bushes had grown so thick that I could scarcely make my way between them, and sometimes the road broadened out into a green, and in one valley a brook, spanned by an old wooden bridge, ran across it. I was tired, and I found a soft and shady place beneath an ash tree, where I must have slept for many hours, for when I woke up it was late in the afternoon. So I went on again, and at last the green road came out into the highway, and I looked up and saw another town on a high place with a great church in the middle of it, and when I went up to it there was a great organ sounding from within, and the choir was singing."

There was a rapture in Darnell's voice as he spoke, that made his story well-nigh swell into a song, and he drew a long breath as the words ended, filled with the thought of that far-off summer day, when some enchantment had informed all common things, transmuting them into a great sacrament, causing earthly works to glow with the fire and the glory of the everlasting light.

And some splendor of that light shone on the face of Mary as she sat still against the sweet gloom of the night, her dark hair making her face more radiant. She was silent for a little while, and then she spoke — "Oh, my dear, why have you waited so long to tell me these wonderful things? I think it is beautiful. Please go on."

"I have always been afraid it was all nonsense," said Darnell. "And I don't know how to explain what I feel. I didn't think I could say so much as I have tonight."

"And did you find it the same day after day?"

"All through the tour? Yes, I think every journey was a success. Of course, I didn't go so far afield every day; I was too tired. Often I rested all day long, and went out in the evening, after the lamps were lit, and then only for a mile or two. I would roam about old, dim squares, and hear the wind from the bills whispering in the trees; and when I knew I was within call of some great glittering street, I was sunk in the silence of ways where I was almost the only passenger, and the lamps were so few and faint that they seemed to give out shadows instead of light. And I would walk slowly, to and fro, perhaps for an hour at a time, in such dark streets, and all the time I felt what I told you about its being my secret — that the shadow, and the dim lights, and the cool of the evening, and trees that were like dark low clouds were all mine, and mine alone, that I was living in a world that nobody else knew of, into which no one could enter.

"I remembered one night I had gone farther. It was somewhere in the far west, where there are orchards and gardens, and great broad lawns that slope down to trees by the river. A great red moon rose that night through mists of sunset, and thin, filmy clouds, and I wandered by a road that passed through the orchards, till I came to a little hill, with the moon showing above it glowing like a great rose. Then I saw figures pass between me and the moon, one by one, in a long line, each bent double, with great packs upon their shoulders. One of them was singing, and then in the middle of the song I heard a horrible shrill laugh, in the thin cracked voice of a very old woman, and they disappeared into the shadow of the trees. I suppose they were people going to work, or coming from work in the gardens; but how like it was to a nightmare!

"I can't tell you about Hampton; I should never finish talking. I was there one evening, not long before they closed the gates, and there were very few people about. But the grey-red, silent, echoing courts, and the flowers falling into dreamland as the night came on, and the dark yews and shadowy-looking statues, and the far, still stretches of water beneath the avenues; and all melting into a blue mist, all being hidden from one s eyes, slowly, surely, as if veils were dropped, one by one, on a great ceremony! Oh! my dear, what could it mean? Far away, across the river, I heard a soft bell ring three times, and three times, and again three times, and I turned away, and my eyes were full of tears.

"I didn't know what it was when I came to it; I only

found out afterward that it must have been Hampton Court. One of the men in the office told me he had taken an A. B. C. girl there, and they had great fun. They got into the maze and couldn't get out again, and then they went on the river and were nearly drowned. He told me there were some spicy pictures in the galleries; his girl shrieked with laughter, so he said."

Mary quite disregarded this interlude.

"But you told me you had made a map. What was it like?"

"I'll show it you some day, if you want to see it. I marked down all the places I had gone to, and made signs — things like queer letters — to remind me of what I had seen. Nobody but myself could understand it. I wanted to draw pictures, but I never learnt how to draw, so when I tried nothing was like what I wanted it to be. I tried to draw a picture of that town on the bill that I came to on the evening of the first day; I wanted to make a steep hill with houses on top, and in the middle, but high above them, the great church, all spires and pinnacles, and above it, in the air, a cup with rays coming from it. But it wasn't a success. I made a very strange sign for Hampton Court, and gave it a name that I made up out of my head."

The Darnells avoided one another's eyes as they sat at breakfast the next morning. The air had lightened in the night, for rain had fallen at dawn; and there was a bright blue sky, with vast white clouds rolling across it from the southwest, and a fresh and joyous wind blew in at the open window; the mists had vanished. And with the mists there seemed to have vanished also the sense of strange things that had possessed Mary and her husband the night before; and as they looked out into the clear light they could scarcely believe that the one had spoken and the other had listened a few hours before to histories very far removed from the usual current of their thoughts and of their lives. They glanced shyly at one another, and spoke of common things, of the question whether Alice would be corrupted by the insidious Mrs. Murry, or whether Mrs. Darnell would be able to persuade the girl that the old woman must be actuated by the worst motives.

"And I think, if I were you," said Darnell, as he went out, "I should step over to the stores and complain of their meat. That last piece of beef was very far from being up to the mark — full of sinew."

III

*I*t might have been different in the evening, and Darnell had matured a plan by which he hoped to gain much. He intended to ask his wife if she would mind having only one gas, and that a good deal lowered, on the pretext that his eyes were tired with work; he thought many things might happen if the room were dimly lit, and the window opened, so that they could sit and watch the night, and listen to the rustling murmur of the tree on the lawn. But his plans were made in vain, for when he got to the garden gate his wife, in tears, came forth to meet him.

"Oh, Edward," she began, "such a dreadful thing has happened! I never liked him much, but I didn't think he would ever do such awful things."

"What do you mean? Who are you talking about? What has happened? Is it Alice's young man?"

"No, no. But come in, dear. I can see that woman opposite watching us: she's always on the look out."

"Now, what is it?" said Darnell, as they sat down to tea. "Tell me, quick! you've quite frightened me."

"I don't know how to begin, or where to start. Aunt Marian has thought that there was something queer for weeks. And then she found — oh, well, the long and short of it is that Uncle Robert has been carrying on dreadfully with some horrid girl, and aunt has found out everything!"

"Lord! you don't say so! The old rascal! Why, he must be nearer seventy than sixty!"

"He's just sixty-five; and the money he has given her —"

The first shock of surprise over, Darnell turned resolutely to his mince.

"We'll have it all out after tea," he said; "I am not going to have my meals spoilt by that old fool of a Nixon. Fill up my cup, will you, dear?"

"Excellent mince this," he went on, calmly. "A little lemon juice and a bit of ham in it? I thought there was something extra. Alice all right today? That's good. I expect she's getting over all that nonsense."

He went on calmly chattering in a manner that astonished Mrs. Darnell, who felt that by the fall of Uncle Robert the natural order had been inverted, and had scarcely touched food since the intelligence had arrived by the second post. She had started out to keep the appointment her aunt had made early in the morning, and had spent most of the day in a first-class waiting-room at Victoria Station, where she had heard all the story.

"Now," said Darnell, when the table had been cleared, "tell us all about it. How long has it been going on?"

"Aunt thinks now, from little things she remembers, that it must have been going on for a year at least. She says there has been a horrid kind of mystery about uncle's behavior for a long time, and her nerves were quite shaken, as she thought he must be involved with Anarchists, or something dreadful of the sort."

"What on earth made her think that?"

"Well, you see, once or twice when she was out walking with her husband, she has been startled by whistles, which seemed to follow them everywhere. You know there are some nice country walks at Barnet, and one in particular, in the fields near Totteridge, that uncle and aunt rather made a point of going to on fine Sunday evenings. Of course, this was not the first thing she noticed, but, at the time, it made a great impression on her mind; she could hardly get a wink of sleep for weeks and weeks."

"Whistling?" said Darnell. "I don't quite understand. Why should she be frightened by whistling?"

"I'll tell you. The first time it happened was one Sunday in last May. Aunt had a fancy they were being followed a Sunday or two before, but she didn't see or hear anything, except a sort of crackling noise in the hedge. But this particular Sunday they had hardly got through the stile into the fields, when she heard a peculiar kind of low whistle. She took no notice, thinking it was no concern of hers or her husband's, but as they went on she heard it again, and then again, and it followed them the whole walk, and it made her so uncomfortable, because she didn't know where it was coming from or who was doing it, or why. Then, just as they got out of the fields into the lane, uncle said he felt quite faint, and he thought he would try a little brandy at the 'Turpin's Head,' a small public-house there is there. And she looked at him and saw his face was quite purple — more like apoplexy, as she says, than fainting fits, which make people look a sort of greenish-white. But she said nothing, and thought perhaps uncle had a peculiar way of fainting of his own, as he always was a man to have his own way of doing everything. So she just waited in the road, and he went ahead and slipped into the public, and aunt says she thought she saw a little figure rise out of the dusk and slip in after him, but she couldn't be sure. And when uncle came out he looked red instead of purple, and said he felt much better; and so they went borne quietly together, and nothing more was said. You see, uncle had said nothing about the whistling, and aunt had been so frightened that she didn't dare speak, for fear they might be both shot.

"She wasn't thinking anything more about it, when two Sundays afterward the very same thing happened just as it had before. This time aunt plucked up a spirit, and asked uncle what it could be. And what do you think he said? 'Birds, my dear, birds.' Of course aunt said to him that no bird that ever flew with wings made a noise like that: sly, and low, with pauses in between; and then he said that many rare sorts of birds lived in North Middlesex and Hertfordshire. 'Nonsense, Robert,' said aunt, 'how can you talk so, considering it has followed us all the way, for a mile or more?' And then uncle told her that some birds were so attached to man that "they would follow one about for miles sometimes; he said he had just been reading about a bird like that in a book of travels. And do you know that when they got home he actually showed her a piece in the 'Hertfordshire Naturalist' which they took in to oblige a friend of theirs, all about rare birds found in the neighborhood, all the most outlandish names, aunt says, that she had never heard or thought of, and uncle had the impudence to say that it must have been a

Purple Sandpiper, which, the paper said, had 'a low shrill note, constantly repeated.' And then he took down a book of Siberian Travels from the bookcase and showed her a page which told how a man was followed by a bird all day long through a forest. And that's what Aunt Marian says vexes her more than anything almost; to think that he should be so artful and ready with those books, twisting them to his own wicked ends. But, at the time, when she was out walking, she simply couldn't make out what he meant by talking about birds in that random, silly sort of way, so unlike him, and they went on, that horrible whistling following them, she looking straight ahead and walking fast, really feeling more huffy and put out than frightened. And when they got to the next stile, she got over and turned round, and 'lo and behold,' as she says, there was no Uncle Robert to be seen! She felt herself go quite white with alarm, thinking of that whistle, and making sure he'd been spirited away or snatched in some way or another, and she had just screamed out 'Robert' like a mad woman, when he came quite slowly round the corner, as cool as a cucumber, holding something in his hand. He said there were some flowers he could never pass, and when aunt saw that he had got a dandelion torn up by the roots, she felt as if her head were going round."

Mary's story was suddenly interrupted. For ten minutes Darnell had been writhing in his chair, suffering tortures in his anxiety to avoid wounding his wife's feelings, but the episode of the dandelion was too much for him, and he burst into a long, wild shriek of laughter, aggravated by suppression into the semblance of a Red Indian's war-whoop. Alice, who was washing-up n the scullery, dropped some three shillings' worth of china, and the neighbors ran out into their gardens wondering if it were murder. Mary gazed reproachfully at her husband.

"How can you be so unfeeling, Edward?" she said, at length, when Darnell had passed into the feebleness of exhaustion. "If you had seen the tears rolling down poor Aunt Marian's cheeks as she told me, I don't think you would have laughed. I didn't think you were so hard-hearted."

"My dear Mary," said Darnell, faintly, through sobs and catching of the breath, "I am awfully sorry. I know it's very sad, really, and I'm not unfeeling; but it is such an odd tale, now, isn't it?

The Sandpiper, you know, and then the dandelion!"

His face twitched and he ground his teeth together. Mary looked gravely at him for a moment, and then she put her hands to her face, and Darnell could see that she also shook with merriment. "I am as bad as you," she said, at last. "I never thought of it in that way. I'm glad I didn't, or I should have laughed in Aunt Marian's face, and I wouldn't have done that for the world. Poor old thing; she cried as if her heart would break. I met her at Victoria, as she asked me, and we had some soup at a confectioner's. I could scarcely touch it; her tears kept dropping into the plate all the time; and then we went to the waiting-room at the station, and she cried there terribly."

"Well," said Darnell, "what happened next? I won't laugh anymore.

"No, we mustn't; it's much too horrible for a joke. Well, of course aunt went home and wondered and wondered what could be the matter, and tried to think it out, but, as she says, she could make nothing of it. She began to be afraid that uncle's brain was giving way through overwork, as he had stopped in the City (as he said) up to all hours lately, and he had to go to Yorkshire (wicked old story-teller!), about some very tiresome business connected with his leases. But then she reflected that however queer he might be getting, even his queerness couldn't make whistles in the air, though, as she said, he was always a wonderful man. So she had to give that up; and then she wondered if there were anything the matter with her, as she had read about people who heard noises when there was really nothing at all. But that wouldn't do either, because though it might account for the whistling, it wouldn't account for the dandelion or the Sandpiper, or for fainting fits that turned purple, or any of uncle's queerness. So aunt said she could think of nothing but to read the Bible every day from the beginning, and by the time she got into Chronicles she felt rather better, especially as nothing had happened for three or four Sundays. She noticed uncle seemed absent-minded, and not as nice to her as he might be, but she put that down to too much work, as he never came home before the last train, and had a hansom twice all the way, getting there between three and four in the morning. Still, she felt it was no good bothering her head over what couldn't be made out or explained anyway, and she was just settling down, when one Sunday evening it began all over again, and worse things happened. The whistling followed them just as it did before, and poor aunt set her teeth and said nothing to uncle, as she knew he would only tell her stories, and they were walking on, not saying a word, when something made her look back, and there was a horrible boy with red hair, peeping through the hedge just behind, and grinning. She said it was a dreadful face, with something unnatural about it, as if it had been a dwarf, and before she had time to have a good look, it popped back like lightning, and aunt all but fainted away."

"A red-headed *boy*?" said Darnell. "I thought — What an extraordinary story this is. I've never heard of anything so queer. Who was the boy?"

"You will know in good time," said Mrs. Darnell. "It *is* very strange, isn't it?"

"Strange!" Darnell ruminated for a while.

"I know what I think, Mary," he said at length. "I don't believe a word of it. I believe your aunt is going mad, or has gone mad, and that she has delusions. The whole thing sounds to me like the invention of a lunatic."

"You are quite wrong. Every word is true, and if you will let me go on, you will understand how it all happened."

"Very good, go ahead."

"Let me see, where was I? Oh, I know, aunt saw the boy grinning in the hedge. Yes, well, she was dreadfully frightened for a minute or two; there was something so queer about the face, but then she plucked up a spirit and said to herself, 'After all, better a boy with red hair than a big man with a gun,' and she made up her mind to watch Uncle Robert closely, as she could see by his look he knew all about it; he seemed as if he were thinking hard and puzzling over something, as if he didn't know what to do next, and his mouth kept opening and shutting, like a fish's. So she kept her face straight, and didn't say a word, and when he said something to her about the fine sunset, she took no notice. 'Don't you hear what I say, Marian?' he said, speaking quite crossly, and bellowing as if it were to somebody in the next field. So aunt said she was very sorry, but her cold made her so deaf, she couldn't hear much. She noticed uncle looked quite pleased, and relieved too, and she knew he thought she hadn't heard the whistling. Suddenly uncle pretended to see a beautiful spray of honeysuckle high up in the hedge, and he said he must get it for aunt, only she must go on ahead, as it made him nervous to be watched. She said she would, but she Just stepped aside behind a bush where there was a sort of cover in the hedge, and found she could see him quite well, though she scratched her face terribly with poking it into a rose bush. And in a minute or two out came the boy from behind the hedge, and she saw uncle and him talking, and she knew it was the same boy, as it wasn't dark enough to hide his flaming red head. And uncle put out his hand as if to catch him, but he just darted into the bushes and vanished. Aunt never said a word at the time, but that night when they got home she charged uncle with what she'd seen and asked him what it all meant. He was quite taken aback at first, and stammered and stuttered and said a spy wasn't his notion of a good wife, but at last he made her swear secrecy, and told her that he was a very high Freemason, and that the boy was an emissary of the order who brought him messages of the greatest importance. But aunt didn't believe a word of it, as an uncle of hers was a mason, and he never behaved like that. It was then she began to be afraid that it was really Anarchists, or something of the kind, and every time the bell rang she thought that uncle had been found out, and the police had come for him."

"What nonsense! As if a man with house property would be an Anarchist."

"Well, she could see there must be some horrible secret, and she didn't know what else to think. And then she began to have the things through the post."

"Things through the post! What do you mean by that?"

"All sorts of things; bits of broken bottle-glass, packed carefully as if it were jewelry; parcels that unrolled and unrolled worse than Chinese boxes, and then had 'cat' in large letters when you came to the middle; old artificial teeth, a cake of red paint, and at last cockroaches."

"Cockroaches by post! Stuff and nonsense; your aunt's mad."

"Edward, she showed me the box; it was made to hold cigarettes, and there were three dead cockroaches inside. And when she found a box of exactly the same kind, half-full of cigarettes, in uncle's great-coat pocket, then her head began to turn again."

Darnell groaned, and stirred uneasily in his chair, feeling that the tale of Aunt Marian's domestic troubles was putting on the semblance of an evil dream.

"Anything else?" he asked.

"My dear, I haven't repeated half the things poor aunt told me this afternoon. There was the night she thought she saw a ghost in the shrubbery. She was anxious about some chickens that were just due to hatch out, so she went out after dark with some egg and bread-crumbs, in case they might be out. And just before her she saw a figure gliding by the rhododendrons. It looked like a short, slim man dressed as they used to be hundreds of years ago; she saw the sword by his side, and the feather in his cap. She thought she should have died, she said, and though it was gone in a minute, and she tried to make out it was all her fancy, she fainted when she got into the house. Uncle was at home that night, and when she came to and told him he ran out, and stayed out for half-an-hour or more, and then came in and said he could find nothing; and the next minute aunt heard that low whistle just outside the window, and uncle ran out again."

"My dear Mary, do let us come to the point. What on earth does it all lead to?"

"Haven't you guessed? Why, of course it was that girl all the time.

"Girl? I thought you said it was a boy with a red head?"

"Don't you see? She's an actress, and she dressed up.

She won't leave uncle alone. It wasn't enough that he was with her nearly every evening in the week, but she must be after him on Sundays too. Aunt found a letter the horrid thing had written, and so it has all come out. Enid Vivian she calls herself, though I don't suppose she has any right to one name or the other. And the question is, what is to be done?"

"Let us talk of that again. I'll have a pipe, and then we'll go to bed."

They were almost asleep when Mary said suddenly — "Doesn't it seem queer, Edward? Last night you were telling me such beautiful things, and tonight I have been talking about that disgraceful old man and his goings on."

"I don't know," answered Darnell, dreamily. "On the walls of that great church upon the hill I saw all kinds of strange grinning monsters, carved in stone."

The misdemeanors of Mr. Robert Nixon brought in their train consequences strange beyond imagination. It was not that they continued to develop on the somewhat fantastic lines of these first adventures which Mrs. Darnell had related; indeed, when "Aunt Marian" came over to Shepherd's Bush, one Sunday afternoon, Darnell wondered how he had had the heart to laugh at the misfortunes of a broken-hearted woman.

He had never seen his wife's aunt before, and he was strangely surprised when Alice showed her into the garden where they were sitting on the warm and misty Sunday in September. To him, save during these latter days, she had always been associated with ideas of splendor and success: his wife had always mentioned the Nixons with a tinge of reverence; he had heard, many times, the epic of Mr. Nixon's struggles and of his slow but triumphant rise. Mary had told the story as she had received it from her parents, beginning with

the flight to London from some small, dull, and un-
prosperous town in the flattest of the Midlands, long
ago, when a young man from the country had great
chances of fortune. Robert Nixon's father had been a
grocer in the High Street, and in after days the successful coal merchant and builder loved to tell of that dull
provincial life, and while he glorified his own victories,
he gave his hearers to understand that he came of a
race which had also known how to achieve. That had
been long ago, he would explain: in the days when that
rare citizen who desired to go to London or to York
was forced to rise in the dead of night, and make his
way, somehow or other, by ten miles of quagmirish,
wandering lanes to the Great North Road, there to
meet the "Lightning" coach, a vehicle which stood to
all the countryside as the visible and tangible embodi-
ment of tremendous speed — "and indeed," as Nixon
would add, "it was always up to time, which is more
than can be said of the Dunham Branch Line nowa-
days!" It was in this ancient Dunham that the Nixons
had waged successful trade for perhaps a hundred
years, in a shop with bulging bay windows looking on
the marketplace. There was no competition, and the
townsfolk, and well-to-do farmers, the clergy and the
country families, looked upon the house of Nixon as
an institution fixed as the town hall (which stood on
Roman pillars) and the parish church. But the change
came: the railway crept nearer and nearer, the farmers
and the country gentry became less well-to-do; the
tanning, which was the local industry, suffered from a
great business which had been established in a larger
town, some twenty miles away, and the profits of the
Nixons grew less and less. Hence the hegira of Robert,
and he would dilate on the poorness of his beginnings,
how he saved, by little and little, from his sorry wage
of City clerk, and how he and a fellow clerk, "who had

come into a hundred pounds," saw an opening in the coal trade — and filled it. It was at this stage of Robert's fortunes, still far from magnificent, that Miss Marian Reynolds had encountered him, she being on a visit to friends in Gunnersbury. Afterward, victory followed victory; Nixon's wharf became a landmark to bargemen; his power stretched abroad, his dusky fleets went outward to the sea, and inward by all the far reaches of canals. Lime, cement, and bricks were added to his merchandise, and at last be hit upon the great stroke — that extensive taking up of land in the north of London. Nixon himself ascribed this *coup* to native sagacity, and the possession of capital; and there were also obscure rumors to the effect that someone or other had been "done" in the course of the transaction. However that might be, the Nixons grew wealthy to excess, and Mary had often told her husband of the state in which they dwelt, of their livened servants, of the glories of their drawing room, of their broad lawn, shadowed by a splendid and ancient cedar. And so Darnell had somehow been led into conceiving the lady of this demesne as a personage of no small pomp. He saw her, tall, of dignified port and presence, inclining, it might be, to some measure of obesity, such a measure as was not unbefitting in an elderly lady of position, who lived well and lived at ease. He even imagined a slight ruddiness of complexion, which went very well with hair that was beginning to turn grey, and when he heard the door-bell ring, as he sat under the mulberry on the Sunday afternoon, he bent forward to catch sight of this stately figure, clad, of course, in the richest, blackest silk, girt about with heavy chains of gold.

He started with amazement when he saw the strange presence that followed the servant into the garden. Mrs. Nixon was a little, thin old woman, who bent as

she feebly trotted after Alice; her eyes were on the
ground, and she did not lift them when the Darnells
rose to greet her. She glanced to the right, uneasily, as
she shook hands with Darnell, to the left when Mary
kissed her, and when she was placed on the garden seat
with a cushion at her back, she looked away at the back
of the houses in the next street. She was dressed in
black, it was true, but even Darnell could see that her
gown was old and shabby, that the fur trimming of
her cape and the fur boa which was twisted about her
neck were dingy and disconsolate, and had all the
melancholy air which fur wears when it is seen in a
second-hand clothes-shop in a back street. And her
gloves — they were black kid, wrinkled with much wean,
faded to a bluish hue at the fingertips, which showed
signs of painful mending. Her hair, plastered over her
forehead, looked dull and colorless, though some
greasy matter had evidently been used with a view of
producing a becoming gloss, and on it perched an
antique bonnet, adorned with black pendants that
rattled paralytically one against the other.

And there was nothing in Mrs. Nixon's face to
correspond with the imaginary picture that Darnell
had made of her. She was sallow, wrinkled, pinched;
her nose ran to a sharp point, and her red-rimmed eyes
were a queer water-grey, that seemed to shrink alike
from the light and from encounter with the eyes of
others. As she sat beside his wife on the green garden-
seat, Darnell, who occupied a wicker-chair brought out
from the drawing room, could not help feeling that
this shadowy and evasive figure, muttering replies to
Mary's polite questions, was almost impossibly remote
from his conceptions of the rich and powerful aunt,
who could give away a hundred pounds as a mere
birthday gift. She would say little at first; yes, she was
feeling rather tired, it had been so hot all the way, and

she had been afraid to put on lighter things as one never knew at this time of year what it might be like in the evenings; there were apt to be cold mists when the sun went down, and she didn't care to risk bronchitis.

"I thought I should never get here," she went on, raising her voice to an odd querulous pipe. "I'd no notion it was such an out-of-the-way place, it's so many years since I was in this neighborhood."

She wiped her eyes, no doubt thinking of the early days at Turnham Green, when she married Nixon; and when the pocket-handkerchief had done its office she replaced it in a shabby black bag which she clutched rather than carried. Darnell noticed, as he watched her, that the bag seemed full, almost to bursting, and he speculated idly as to the nature of its contents: correspondence, perhaps, he thought, further proofs of Uncle Robert's treacherous and wicked dealings. He grew quite uncomfortable, as he sat and saw her glancing all the while furtively away from his wife and himself, and presently he got up and strolled away to the other end of the garden, where he lit his pipe and walked to and fro on the gravel walk, still astounded at the gulf between the real and the imagined woman.

Presently he heard a hissing whisper, and he saw Mrs. Nixon's head inclining to his wife's. Mary rose and came toward him.

"Would you mind sitting in the drawing room, Edward?" she murmured. "Aunt says she can't bring herself to discuss such a delicate matter before you. I dare say it's quite natural."

"Very well, but I don't thing I'll go into the drawing room. I feel as if a walk would do me good. You mustn't be frightened if I am a little late," he said; "if I don't get back before your aunt goes, say good-bye to her for me."

He strolled into the main road, where the trains were humming to and fro. He was still confused and perplexed, and he tried to account for a certain relief he felt in removing himself from the presence of Mrs. Nixon. He told himself that her grief at her husband's ruffianly conduct was worthy of all pitiful respect, but at the same time, to his shame, he had felt a certain physical aversion from her as she sat in his garden in her dingy black, dabbing her red-rimmed eyes with a damp pocket-handkerchief. He had been to the Zoo when he was a lad, and he still remembered how he had shrunk with horror at the sight of certain reptiles slowly crawling over one another in their slimy pond. But he was enraged at the similarity between the two sensations, and he walked briskly on that level and monotonous road, looking about him at the unhandsome spectacle of suburban London keeping Sunday.

There was something in the tinge of antiquity which still exists in Acton that soothed his mind and drew it away from those unpleasant contemplations, and when at last he had penetrated rampant after rampart of brick, and heard no more the harsh shrieks and laughter of the people who were enjoying themselves, he found a way into a little sheltered field, and sat down in peace beneath a tree, whence he could look out on a pleasant valley. The sun sank down beneath the hills, the clouds changed into the likeness of blossoming rose-gardens; and he still sat there in the gathering darkness till a cool breeze blew upon him, and he rose with a sigh, and turned back to the brick ramparts and the glimmering streets, and the noisy idlers sauntering to and fro in the procession of their dismal festival. But he was murmuring to himself some words that seemed a magic song, and it was with uplifted heart that he let himself into his house.

Mrs. Nixon had gone an hour and a half before his

return, Mary told him. Darnell sighed with relief, and he and his wife strolled out into the garden and sat down side by side.

They kept silence for a time, and at last Mary spoke, not without a nervous tremor in her voice. "I must tell you, Edward," she began, "that aunt has made a proposal which you ought to hear. I think we should consider it."

"A proposal? But how about the whole affair? Is it still going on?"

"Oh, yes! She told me all about it. Uncle is quite unrepentant. It seems he has taken a flat somewhere in town for that woman, and furnished it in the most costly manner. He simply laughs at aunt's reproaches, and says he means to have some fun at last. You saw how broken she was?"

"Yes; very sad. But won't he give her any money? Wasn't she very badly dressed for a woman in her position?"

"Aunt has no end of beautiful things, but I fancy she likes to hoard them; she has a horror of spoiling her dresses. It isn't for want of money, I assure you, as uncle settled a very large sum on her two years ago, when he was everything that could be desired as a husband. And that brings me to what I want to say. Aunt would like to live with us. She would pay very liberally. What do you say?"

"Would like to live with us?" exclaimed Darnell, and his pipe dropped from his hand on to the grass. He was stupefied by the thought of Aunt Marian as a boarder, and sat staring vacantly before him, wondering what new monster the night would next produce.

"I knew you wouldn't much like the idea," his wife went on. "But I do think, dearest, that we ought not to refuse without very serious consideration. I am afraid you did not take to poor aunt very much."

Darnell shook his head dumbly.

"I thought you didn't; she was so upset, poor thing, and you didn't see her at her best. She is really so good. But listen to me, dear. Do you think we have the right to refuse her offer? I told you she has money of her own, and I am sure she would be dreadfully offended if we said we wouldn't have her. And what would become of me if anything happened to you? You know we have very little saved."

Darnell groaned.

"It seems to me," he said, "that it would spoil everything. We are so happy, Mary dear, by ourselves. Of course I am extremely sorry for your aunt. I think she is very much to be pitied. But when it comes to having her always here —"

"I know, dear. Don't think I am looking forward to the prospect; you know I don't want anybody but you. Still, we ought to think of the future, and besides we shall be able to live so very much better. I shall be able to give you all sorts of nice things that I know you ought to have after all that hard work in the City. Our income would be doubled."

"Do you mean she would pay us £150 a year?"

"Certainly. And she would pay for the spare room being furnished, and any extra she might want. She told me, specially, that if a friend or two came now and again to see her, she would gladly bear the cost of a fire in the drawing room, and give something toward the gas bill, with a few shillings for the girl for any additional trouble. We should certainly be more than twice as well off as we are now. You see, Edward, dear, it's not the sort of offer we are likely to have again. Besides, we must think of the future, as I said. Do you know aunt took a great fancy to you?"

He shuddered and said nothing, and his wife went on with her argument.

"And, you see, it isn't as if we should see so very much of her. She will have her breakfast in bed, and she told me she would often go up to her room in the evening directly after dinner. I thought that very nice and considerate. She quite understands that we shouldn't like to have a third person always with us. Don't you think, Edward, that, considering everything, we ought to say we will have her?"

"Oh, I suppose so," he groaned. "As you say, it's a very good offer, financially, and I am afraid it would be very imprudent to refuse. But I don't like the notion, I confess."

"I am so glad you agree with me, dear. Depend upon it, it won't be half so bad as you think. And putting our own advantage on one side, we shall really be doing poor aunt a very great kindness. Poor old dear, she cried bitterly after you were gone; she said she had made up her mind not to stay any longer in Uncle Robert's house, and she didn't know where to go, or what would become of her, if we refused to take her in. She quite broke down."

"Well, well; we will try it for a year, anyhow. It may be as you say; we shan't find it quite so bad as it seems now. Shall we go in?"

He stooped for his pipe, which lay as it had fallen, on the grass. He could not find it, and lit a wax match which showed him the pipe, and close beside it, under the seat, something that looked like a page torn from a book. He wondered what it could be, and picked it up.

The gas was lit in the drawing room, and Mrs. Darnell, who was arranging some notepaper, wished to write at once to Mrs. Nixon, cordially accepting her proposal, when she was startled by an exclamation from her husband.

"What is the matter?" she said, startled by the tone

of his voice. "You haven't hurt yourself?"

"Look at this," he replied, handing her a small leaflet; "I found it under the garden seat just now."

Mary glanced with bewilderment at her husband and read as follows:

THE NEW AND CHOSEN SEED
OF ABRAHAM
PROPHECIES TO BE FULFILLED IN
THE PRESENT YEAR

1. The Sailing of a Fleet of One hundred and Forty and Four Vessels for Tarshish and the Isles.

2. Destruction of the Power of the Dog, including all the instruments of anti-Abrahamic legislation.

3. Return of the Fleet from Tarshish, bearing with it the gold of Arabia, destined to be the Foundation of the New City of Abraham.

4. The Search for the Bride, and the bestowing of the Seals on the Seventy and Seven.

5. The Countenance of FATHER to become luminous, but with a greater glory than the face of Moses.

6. The Pope of Rome to be stoned with stones in the valley called Berek-Zittor.

7. FATHER to be acknowledged by Three Great Rulers. Two Great Rulers will deny FATHER, and will immediately perish in the Effluvia of FATHER's Indignation.

8. Binding of the Beast with the Little Horn, and all Judges cast down.

9. Finding of the Bride in the Land of Egypt, which has been revealed to FATHER as now existing in the western part of London.

10. Bestowal of the New Tongue on the Seventy and Seven, and on the One Hundred and Forty

and Four. FATHER proceeds to the Bridal Chamber.

11. Destruction of London and rebuilding of the City called No, which is the New City of Abraham.

12. FATHER united to the Bride, and the present Earth removed to the Sun for the space of half an hour.

Mrs. Darnell's brow cleaned as she read matter which seemed to her harmless if incoherent. From her husband's voice she had been led to fear something more tangibly unpleasant than a vague catena of prophecies.

"Well," she said, "what about it?"

"What about it? Don't you see that your aunt dropped it, and that she must be a raging lunatic?"

"Oh, Edward! don't say that. In the first place, how do you know that aunt dropped it at all? It might easily have blown over from any of the other gardens. . And, if it were hers, I don't think you should call her a lunatic. I don't believe, myself, that there are any real prophets now; but there are many good people who think quite differently. I knew an old lady once who, I am sure, was very good, and she took in a paper every week that was full of prophecies and things very like this. Nobody called her mad, and I have heard father say that she had one of the sharpest heads for business he had ever come across."

"Very good; have it as you like. But I believe we shall both be sorry."

They sat in silence for some time. Alice came in after her "evening out," and they sat on, till Mrs. Darnell said she was tired and wanted to go to bed.

Her husband kissed her. "I don't think I will come up just yet," he said; "you go to sleep, dearest. I want to think things over. No, no; I am not going to change my mind: your aunt shall come, as I said. But there are one or two things I should like to get settled in my mind."

He meditated for a long while, pacing up and down the room. Light after light was extinguished in Edna Road, and the people of the suburb slept all around him, but still the gas was alight in Darnell's drawing room, and he walked softly up and down the floor. He was thinking that about the life of Mary and himself, which had been so quiet, there seemed to be gathering on all sides grotesque and fantastic shapes, omens of confusion and disorder, threats of madness; a strange company from another world. It was as if into the quiet, sleeping streets of some little ancient town among the hills there had come from afar the sound of drum and pipe, snatches of wild song, and there had burst into the marketplace the mad company of the players, strangely bedizened, dancing a furious measure to their hurrying music, drawing forth the citizens from their sheltered homes and peaceful lives, and alluring them to mingle in the significant figures of their dance.

Yet afar and near (for it was hidden in his heart) he beheld the glimmer of a sure and constant star. Beneath, darkness came on, and mists and shadows closed about the town. The red, flickering flame of torches was kindled in the midst of it. The song grew louder, with more insistent, magical tones, surging and falling in unearthly modulations, the very speech of incantation; and the drum beat madly, and the pipe shrilled to a scream, summoning all to issue forth, to leave their peaceful hearths; for a strange rite was preconized in their midst. The streets that Were wont to be so still, so hushed with the cool and tranquil veils of darkness, asleep beneath the patronage of the evening star, now danced with glimmering lanterns, resounded with the cries of those who hurried forth,

drawn as by a magistral spell; and the songs swelled
and triumphed, the reverberant beating of the drum
grew louder, and in the midst of the awakened town
the players, fantastically arrayed, performed their interlude under the red blaze of torches. He knew not
whether they were players, men that would vanish
suddenly as they came, disappearing by the track that
climbed the hill; or whether they were indeed magi-
cians, workers of great and efficacious spells, who knew
the secret word by which the earth may be transformed
into the hall of Gehenna, so that they that gazed and
listened, as at a passing spectacle, should be entrapped
by the sound and the sight presented to them, should
be drawn into the elaborated figures of that mystic
dance, and so should be whirled away into those un-
ending mazes on the wild hills that were abhorred,
there to wander for evermore.

But Darnell was not afraid, because of the Daystar
that had risen in his heart. It had dwelt there all his
life, and had slowly shone forth with clearer and clearer
light, and he began to see that though his earthly steps
might be in the ways of the ancient town that was beset
by the Enchanters, and resounded with their songs and
their processions, yet he dwelt also in that serene and
secure world of brightness, and from a great and un-
utterable height looked on the confusion of the mortal
pageant, beholding mysteries in which he was no true
actor, hearing magic songs that could by no means
draw him down from the battlements of the high and
holy city.

His heart was filled with a great joy and a great peace
as he lay down beside his wife and fell asleep, and in
the morning, when he woke up, he was glad.

IV

*I*n a haze as of a dream Darnell's thoughts seemed to move through the opening days of the next week. Perhaps nature had not intended that he should be practical or much given to that which is usually called "sound common sense," but his training had made him desirous of good, plain qualities of the mind, and he uneasily strove to account to himself for his strange mood of the Sunday night, as he had often endeavored to interpret the fancies of his boyhood and early manhood. At first he was annoyed by his want of success; the morning paper, which he always secured as the 'bus delayed at Uxbnidge Road Station, fell from his hands unread, while he vainly reasoned, assuring him-self that the threatened incursion of a whimsical old woman, though tiresome enough, was no rational excuse for those curious hours of meditation in which his thoughts seemed to have dressed themselves in unfamiliar, fantastic habits, and to parley with him in a strange speech, and yet a speech that he had understood.

With such arguments he perplexed his mind on the long, accustomed ride up the steep ascent of Holland Park, past the incongruous hustle of Notting Hill Gate, where in one direction a road shows the way to the snug, somewhat faded bowers and retreats of Bayswater, and in another one sees the portal of the murky region of the slums. The customary companions of his morning's journey were in the seats about him; he heard the hum of their talk, as they disputed concerning politics, and the man next to him, who came from Acton, asked him what he thought of the Government now. There was a discussion, and a loud and excited one, just in front, as to whether rhubarb was a fruit or vegetable, and in his ear he heard Redman, who was a near neighbor, praising the economy of "the wife."

"I don't know how she does it. Look here; what do you think we had yesterday? Breakfast: fish-cakes, beautifully fried — rich, you know, lots of herbs, it's a receipt of her aunt's; you should just taste 'em. Coffee, bread, butter, marmalade, and, of course, all the usual etceteras. Dinner: roast beef, Yorkshire, potatoes, greens, and horse-radish sauce, plum tart, cheese. And where will you get a better dinner than that? Well, I call it wonderful, I really do."

But in spite of these distractions he fell into a dream as the 'bus rolled and tossed on its way Cityward, and still he strove to solve the enigma of his vigil of the night before, and as the shapes of trees and green lawns and houses passed before his eyes, and as he saw the procession moving on the pavement, and while the murmur of the streets sounded in his ears, all was to him strange and unaccustomed, as if he moved through the avenues of some city in a foreign land. It was, perhaps, on these mornings, as he rode to his mechanical work, that vague and floating fancies that must have long haunted his brain began to shape themselves, and to put on the form of definite conclusions, from which he could no longer escape, even if he had wished it. Darnell had received what is called a sound commercial education, and would therefore have found very great difficulty in putting into articulate speech any thought that was worth thinking; but he grew certain on these mornings that the "common sense" which he had always heard exalted as man's supremest faculty was, in all probability, the smallest and least-considered item in the equipment of an ant of average intelligence. And with this, as an almost necessary corollary, came a firm belief that the whole fabric of life in which he moved was sunken, past all thinking, in the grossest absurdity; that he and all his friends and acquaintances and fellow-workers were interested in matters in which men were never meant to be interested, were pursuing aims which they were never meant to pursue, were, indeed, much like fair stones of an altar serving as a pigsty wall. Life, it seemed to him, was a great search for — he knew not what; and in the process of the ages one by one the true marks upon the ways had been shattered, on buried, or the meaning of the words had been slowly forgotten; one by one the signs had been turned awry, the true entrances had been thickly overgrown, the very way itself had been diverted from the heights to the depths, till at last the race of pilgrims had become hereditary stone-breakers and ditch-scourers on a track that led to destruction — if it led anywhere at all. Darnell's heart thrilled with a strange and trembling joy, with a sense that was all new, when it came to his mind that this great loss might not be a hopeless one, that perhaps the difficulties were by no means insuperable. It might be, he considered, that the stonebreaker had merely to throw down his hammer and set out, and the way would be plain before him; and a single step would free the delver in rubbish from the foul slime of the ditch.

It was, of course, with difficulty and slowly that these things became clear to him. He was an English City clerk, "flourishing" toward the end of the nineteenth century, and the rubbish heap that had been accumulating for some centuries could not be cleared away in an instant. Again and again the spirit of nonsense that had been implanted in him as in his fellows assured him that the true world was the visible and tangible world, the world in which good and faithful letter-copying was exchangeable for a certain quantum of bread, beef, and house-room, and that the man who copied letters well, did not beat his wife, nor lose money foolishly, was a good man, fulfilling the end for which he had been made. But in spite of these arguments, in spite of their acceptance by all who were about him, he had the grace to perceive the utter falsity and absurdity of the whole position. He was fortunate in his entire ignorance of sixpenny "science," but if the whole library had been projected into his brain it would not have moved him to "deny in the darkness that which he had known in the light." Darnell knew by experience that man is made a mystery for mysteries and visions, for the realization in his consciousness of ineffable bliss, for a great joy that transmutes the whole world, for a joy that surpasses all joys and overcomes all sorrows. He knew this certainly, though he knew it dimly; and he was apart from other men, preparing himself for a great experiment.

With such thoughts as these for his secret and concealed treasure, he was able to bear the threatened invasion of Mrs. Nixon with something approaching indifference. He knew, indeed, that her presence between his wife and himself would be unwelcome to him, and he was not without grave doubts as to the woman's sanity; but after all, what did it matter? Besides, already a faint glimmering light had risen within him that showed the profit of self-negation, and in this matter he had preferred his wife's will to his own. *Et non sua pomo;* to his astonishment he found a delight in denying himself his own wish, a process that he had always regarded as thoroughly detestable. This was a state of things which he could not in the least understand; but, again, though a member of a most hopeless class, living in the most hopeless surroundings that the world has ever seen, though he knew as much of the *askesis* as of Chinese metaphysics; again, he had the grace not to deny the light that had begun to glimmer in his soul.

And he found a present reward in the eyes of Mary, when she welcomed him home after his foolish labors in the cool of the evening. They sat together, hand in hand, under the mulberry tree, at the coming of the dusk, and as the ugly walls about them became obscure and vanished into the formless world of shadows, they seemed to be freed from the bondage of Shepherd's Bush, freed to wander in that undisfigured, undefiled world that lies beyond the walls. Of this region Mary knew little on nothing by experience, since her relations had always been of one mind with the modern world, which has for the true country an instinctive and most significant horror and dread. Mr. Reynolds had also shared in another odd superstition of these later days — that it is necessary to leave London at least once a year; consequently Mary had some knowledge of various seaside resorts on the south and east coasts, where Londoners gather in hordes, turn the sands into one vast, bad music hall, and derive, as they say, enormous benefit from the change. But experiences such as these give but little knowledge of the country in its true and occult sense; and yet Mary, as she sat in the dusk beneath the whispering tree, knew something of the secret of the wood, of the valley shut in by high hills, where the sound of pouring water always echoes from the clear brook. And to Darnell these were nights of great dreams; for it was the hour of the work, the time of transmutation, and he who could not understand the miracle, who could scarcely believe in it, yet knew, secretly and half consciously, that the water was being changed into the wine of a new life. This was ever the inner music of his dreams, and to it he added on these still and sacred nights the far-off memory of that time long ago when, a child, before the world had overwhelmed him, he journeyed down to the old grey house in the west, and for a whole month heard the murmur of the forest through his bedroom window, and when the wind was hushed, the washing of the tides about the needs; and sometimes awaking very early he had heard the strange cry of a bird as it rose from its nest among the needs, and had looked out and had seen the valley whiten to the dawn, and the winding river whiten as it swam down to the sea. The memory of all this had faded and become shadowy as he grew olden and the chains of common life were riveted firmly about his soul; all the atmosphere by which he was surrounded was well-nigh fatal to such thoughts, and only now and again in half-conscious moments or in sleep he had revisited that valley in the far-off west, where the breath of wind was an incantation, and every leaf and stream and hill spoke of great and ineffable mysteries. But now the broken vision was in great part restored to him, and looking with love in his wife's eyes he saw the gleam of water-pools in the still forest, saw the mists rising in the evening, and heard the music of the winding river.

They were sitting thus together on the Friday evening of the week that had begun with that odd and half-forgotten visit of Mrs. Nixon, when, to Darnell's annoyance, the door-bell gave a discordant peal, and Alice with some disturbance of manner came out and announced that a gentleman wished to see the master. Darnell went into the drawing room, where Alice had lit one gas so that it flared and burned with a rushing sound, and in this distorting light there waited a stout, elderly gentleman, whose countenance was altogether unknown to him. He stared blankly, and hesitated, about to speak, but the visitor began.

"You don't know who I am, but I expect you'll know my name. It's Nixon."

He did not wait to be interrupted. He sat down and plunged into narrative, and after the first few words, Darnell, whose mind was not altogether unprepared, listened without much astonishment.

"And the long and the short of it is," Mr. Nixon said at last, "she's gone stark, staring mad, and we had to put her away today — poor thing."

His voice broke a little, and he wiped his eyes hastily, for though stout and successful he was not unfeeling, and he was fond of his wife. He had spoken quickly, and had gone lightly over many details which might have interested specialists in certain kinds of mania, and Darnell was sorry for his evident distress. "I came here," he went on after a brief pause, "because I found out she had been to see you last Sunday, and I knew the sort of story she must have told."

Darnell showed him the prophetic leaflet which Mrs. Nixon had dropped in the garden. "Did you know about this?" he said.

"Oh, *him*," said the old man, with some approach to cheerfulness; "oh yes, I thrashed *him* black and blue the day before yesterday."

"Isn't he mad? Who is the man?"

"He's not mad, he's bad. He's a little Welsh skunk named Richards. He's been running some sort of chapel over at New Barnet for the last few years, and my poor wife — she never could find the parish church good enough for her — had been going to his damned schism shop for the last twelve-month. It was all that finished her off. Yes; I thrashed *him* the day before yesterday, and I'm not afraid of a summons either. I know him, and he knows I know him."

Old Nixon whispered something in Darnell's ear, and chuckled faintly as he repeated for the third time his formula — "I thrashed *him* black and blue the day before yesterday."

Darnell could only murmur condolences and express his hope that Mrs. Nixon might recover. The old man shook his head.

"I'm afraid there's no hope of that," he said. "I've had the best advice, but they couldn't do anything, and told me so."

Presently he asked to see his niece, and Darnell went out and prepared Mary as well as he could. She could scarcely take in the news that her aunt was a hopeless maniac, for Mrs. Nixon, having been extremely stupid all her days, had naturally succeeded in passing with her relations as typically sensible. With the Reynolds family, as with the great majority of us, want of imagination is always equated with sanity, and though many of us have never heard of Lombroso we are his ready-made converts. We have always believed that poets are mad, and if statistics unfortunately show that few poets have really been inhabitants of lunatic asylums, it is soothing to learn that nearly all poets have had whooping-cough, which is doubtless, like intoxication, a minor madness.

"But is it really true?" she asked at length. "Are you certain uncle is not deceiving you? Aunt seemed so sensible always."

She was helped at last by recollecting that Aunt Marian used to get up very early of mornings, and then they went into the drawing room and talked to the old man. His evident kindliness and honesty grew upon Mary, in spite of a lingering belief in her aunt's fables, and when he left, it was with a promise to come to see them again.

Mrs. Darnell said she felt tired, and went to bed; and Darnell returned to the garden and began to pace to and fro, collecting his thoughts. His immeasurable relief at the intelligence that, after all, Mrs. Nixon was not coming to live with them taught him that, despite his submission, his dread of the event had been very great. The weight was removed, and now he was free to consider his life without reference to the grotesque intrusion that he had feared. He sighed for joy, and as he paced to and fro he savored the scent of the night, which, though it came faintly to him in that brick-bound suburb, summoned to his mind across many years the odor of the world at night as he had known it in that short sojourn of his boyhood; the odor that rose from the earth when the flame of the sun had gone down beyond the mountain, and the afterglow had paled in the sky and on the fields. And as he recovered as best he could these lost dreams of an enchanted land, there came to him other images of his childhood, forgotten and yet not forgotten, dwelling unheeded in dark places of the memory, but ready to be summoned forth. He remembered one fantasy that had long haunted him. As he lay half asleep in the forest on one hot afternoon of that memorable visit to the country, he had "made believe" that a little companion had come to him out of the blue mists and the green light beneath the leaves — a white girl with long black hair, who had played with him and whispered her secrets in his ear, as his father lay sleeping under a tree; and from that summer afternoon, day by day, she had been beside him; she had visited him in the wilderness of London, and even in recent years there had come to him now and again the sense of her presence, in the midst of the heat and turmoil of the City. The last visit he remembered well; it was a few weeks before he married, and from the depths of some futile task he had looked up with puzzled eyes, wondering why the close air suddenly grew scented with green leaves, why the murmur of the trees and the wash of the river on the reeds came to his ears; and then that sudden rapture to which he had given a name and an individuality possessed him utterly. He knew then how the dull flesh of man can be like fire; and now, looking back from a new standpoint on this and other experiences, he realized how all that was real in his life had been unwelcomed, uncherished by him, had come to him, perhaps, in virtue of merely negative qualities on his part. And yet, as he reflected, he saw that there had been a chain of witnesses all through his life: again and again voices had whispered in his ear words in a strange language that he now recognized as his native tongue; the common street had not been lacking in visions of the true land of his birth; and in all the passing and repassing of the world he saw that there had been emissaries ready to guide his feet on the way of the great journey.

A week or two after the visit of Mr. Nixon, Dannell took his annual holiday.

There was no question of Walton-on-the-Naze, or of

anything of the kind, as he quite agreed with his wife's longing for some substantial sum put by against the evil day. But the weather was still fine, and he lounged away the time in his garden beneath the tree, or he sauntered out on long aimless walks in the western purlieus of London, not unvisited by that old sense of some great ineffable beauty, concealed by the dim and dingy veils of grey interminable streets. Once, on a day of heavy rain he went to the "box-room," and began to turn over the papers in the old hair trunk — scraps and odds and ends of family history, some of them in his father's handwriting, others in faded ink, and there were a few ancient pocketbooks, filled with manuscript of a still earlier time, and in these the ink was glossier and blacker than any writing fluids supplied by stationers of later days. Darnell had hung up the portrait of the ancestor in this room, and had bought a solid kitchen table and a chair; so that Mrs. Darnell, seeing him looking over his old documents, half thought of naming the room "Mr. Darnell's study." He had not glanced at these relics of his family for many years, but from the hour when the rainy morning sent him to them, he remained constant to research till the end of the holidays. It was a new interest, and he began to fashion in his mind a faint picture of his forefathers, and of their life in that grey old house in the river valley, in the western land of wells and streams and dark and ancient woods. And there were stranger things than mere notes on family history amongst that odd litter of old disregarded papers, and when he went back to his work in the City some of the men fancied that he was in some vague manner changed in appearance; but he only laughed when they asked him where he had been and what he had been doing with himself. But Mary noticed that every evening he spent at least an hour in the box-room; she was rather sorry at the waste of time involved in reading old papers about dead people. And one afternoon, as they were out together on a somewhat dreary walk toward Acton, Darnell stopped at a hopeless secondhand bookshop, and after scanning the rows of shabby books in the window, went in and purchased two volumes. They proved to be a Latin dictionary and grammar, and she was surprised to hear her husband declare his intention of acquiring the Latin language.

But, indeed, all his conduct impressed her as indefinably altered; and she began to be a little alarmed, though she could scarcely have formed her fears in words. But she knew that in some way that was all indefined and beyond the grasp of her thought their lives had altered since the summer, and no single thing wore quite the same aspect as before. If she looked out into the dull street with its rare loiterers, it was the same and yet it had altered, and if she opened the window in the early morning the wind that entered came with a changed breath that spoke some message that she could not understand. And day by day passed by in the old course, and not even the four walls were altogether familiar, and the voices of men and women sounded with strange notes, with the echo, rather, of a music that came over unknown hills. And day by day as she went about her household work, passing from shop to shop in those dull streets that were a network, a fatal labyrinth of grey desolation on every side, there came to her sense half-seen images of some other world, as if she walked in a dream, and every moment must bring her to light and to awakening, when the grey should fade, and regions long desired should appear in glory. Again and again it seemed as if that which was hidden would be shown even to the sluggish testimony of sense; and as she went to and fro from street to street of that dim and weary suburb, and looked on those grey material walls, they seemed as if a light glowed behind them, and again and again the mystic fragrance of incense was blown to her nostrils from across the verge of that world which is not so much impenetrable as ineffable, and to her ears came the dream of a chant that spoke of hidden choirs about all her ways. She struggled against these impressions, refusing her assent to the testimony of them, since all the pressure of credited opinion for three hundred years has been directed toward stamping out real knowledge, and so effectually has this been accomplished that we can only recover the truth through much anguish. And so Mary passed the days in a strange perturbation, clinging to common things and common thoughts, as if she feared that one morning she would wake up in an unknown world to a changed life. And Edward Darnell went day by day to his labor and returned in the evening, always with that shining of light within his eyes and upon his face, with the gaze of wonder that was greater day by day, as if for him the veil grew thin and soon would disappear.

From these great matters both in herself and in her husband Mary shrank back, afraid, perhaps, that if she began the question the answer might be too wonderful. She rather taught herself to be troubled over little things; she asked herself what attraction there could be in the old records over which she supposed Edward to be poring night after night in the cold room upstairs. She had glanced over the papers at Darnell's invitation, and could see but little interest in them; there were one or two sketches, roughly done in pen and ink, of the old house in the west: it looked a shapeless and fantastic place, furnished with strange pillars and stranger ornaments on the projecting porch; and on one side a roof dipped down almost to the earth, and in the center there was something that might almost be a tower rising above the rest of the building. Then there were documents that seemed all names and dates, with here and there a coat of arms done in the margin, and she came upon a string of uncouth Welsh names linked together by the word "ap" in a chain that looked endless. There was a paper covered with signs and figures that meant nothing to her, and then there were the pocketbooks, full of old-fashioned writing, and much of it in Latin, as her husband told her — it was a collection as void of significance as a treatise on conic sections, so far as Mary was concerned. But night after night Darnell shut himself up with the musty rolls, and more than ever when he rejoined her he bore upon his face the blazonry of some great adventure. And one night she asked him what interested him so much in the papers he had shown her.

He was delighted with the question. Somehow they had not talked much together for the last few weeks, and he began to tell her of the records of the old race from which he came, of the old strange house of grey stone between the forest and the river. The family went back and back, he said, far into the dim past, beyond the Normans, beyond the Saxons, far into the Roman days, and for many hundred years they had been petty kings, with a strong fortress high up on the hill, in the heart of the forest; and even now the great mounds remained, whence one could look through the trees toward the mountain on one side and across the yellow sea on the other. The real name of the family was not Darnell; that was assumed by one Iolo ap Taliesin ap Iorwerth in the sixteenth century — why, Darnell did not seem to understand. And then he told her how the race had dwindled in prosperity, century by century, till at last there was nothing left but the grey house and a few acres of land bordering the river.

"And do you know, Mary," he said, "I suppose we

shall go and live there some day or other. My great-uncle, who has the place now, made money in business when he was a young man, and I believe he will leave it all to me. I know I am the only relation he has. How strange it would be. What a change from the life here."

"You never told me that. Don't you think your great-uncle might leave his house and his money to somebody he knows really well? You haven't seen him since you were a little boy, have you?"

"No; but we write once a year. And from what I have heard my father say, I am sure the old man would never leave the house out of the family. Do you think you would like it?"

"I don't know. Isn't it very lonely?"

"I suppose it is. I forget whether there are any other houses in sight, but I don't think there are any at all near. But what a change! No City, no streets, no people passing to and fro; only the sound of the wind and the sight of the green leaves and the green hills, and the song of the voices of the earth." . . . He checked himself suddenly, as if he feared that he was about to tell some secret that must not yet be uttered; and indeed, as he spoke of the change from the little street in Shepherd's Bush to that ancient house in the woods of the far west, a change seemed already to possess himself, and his voice put on the modulation of an antique chant. Mary looked at him steadily and touched his arm, and he drew a long breath before he spoke again.

"It is the old blood calling to the old land," he said. "I was forgetting that I am a clerk in the City."

It was, doubtless, the old blood that had suddenly stirred in him; the resurrection of the old spirit that for many centuries had been faithful to secrets that are now disregarded by most of us, that now day by day was quickened more and more in his heart, and grew so strong that it was hard to conceal. He was indeed almost in the position of the man in the tale, who, by a sudden electric shock, lost the vision of the things about him in the London streets, and gazed instead upon the sea and shone of an island in the Antipodes; for Darnell only clung with an effort to the interests and the atmosphere which, till lately, had seemed all the world to him; and the grey house and the wood and the river, symbols of the other sphere, intruded as it were into the landscape of the London suburb.

But he went on, with more restraint, telling his stories of far-off ancestors, how one of them, the most remote of all, was called a saint, and was supposed to possess certain mysterious secrets often alluded to in the papers as the "Hidden Songs of Iolo Sant." And then with an abrupt transition he recalled memories of his father and of the strange, shiftless life in dingy lodgings in the backwaters of London, of the dim stucco streets that were his first recollections, of forgotten squares in North London, and of the figure of his father, a grave bearded man who seemed always in a dream, as if he too sought for the vision of a land beyond the strong walls, a land where there were deep orchards and many shining hills, and fountains and water-pools gleaming under the leaves of the wood.

"I believe my father earned his living," he went on, "such a living as he did earn, at the Record Office and the British Museum. He used to hunt up things for lawyers and country parsons who wanted old deeds inspected. He never made much, and we were always moving from one lodging to another — always to out-of-the-way places where everything seemed to have run to seed. We never knew our neighbors — we moved too often for that — but my father had about half a dozen friends, elderly men like himself, who used to come to see us pretty often; and then, if there was any money, the lodging-house servant would go out for beer, and they would sit and smoke far into the night.

"I never knew much about these friends of his, but they all had the same look, the look of longing for something hidden. They talked of mysteries that I never understood, very little of their own lives, and when they did speak of ordinary affairs one could tell that they thought such matters as money and the want of it were unimportant trifles. When I grew up and went into the City, and met other young fellows and heard their way of talking, I wondered whether my father and his friends were not a little queer in their heads; but I know better now."

So night after night Darnell talked to his wife, seeming to wander aimlessly from the dingy lodging-houses, where he had spent his boyhood in the company of his father and the other seekers, to the old house hidden in that far western valley, and the old race that had so long looked at the setting of the sun over the mountain. But in truth there was one end in all that he spoke, and Mary felt that beneath his words, however indifferent they might seem, there was hidden a purpose, that they were to embank on a great and marvelous adventure.

So day by day the world became more magical; day by day the work of separation was being performed, the gross accidents were being refined away. Darnell neglected no instruments that might be useful in the work; and now he neither lounged at home on Sunday mornings, nor did he accompany his wife to the Gothic blasphemy which pretended to be a church. They had discovered a little church of another fashion in a back street, and Darnell, who had found in one of the old notebooks the maxim *Incredibilia sola Credenda*, soon perceived how high and glorious a thing was that service at which he assisted. Our stupid ancestors taught us that we could become wise by studying books on "science," by meddling with test-tubes, geological specimens, microscopic preparations, and the like; but they who have cast off these follies know that they must read not "science" books, but mass-books, and that the soul is made wise by the contemplation of mystic ceremonies and elaborate and curious rites. In such things Darnell found a wonderful mystery language, which spoke at once more secretly and more directly than the formal creeds; and he saw that, in a sense, the whole world is but a great ceremony or sacrament, which teaches under visible forms a hidden and transcendent doctrine. It was thus that he found in the ritual of the church a perfect image of the world; an image purged, exalted, and illuminate, a holy house built up of shining and translucent stones, in which the burning torches were more significant than the wheeling stars, and the fuming incense was a more certain token than the rising of the mist. His soul went forth with the albed procession in its white and solemn order, the mystic dance that signifies rapture and a joy above all joys, and when he beheld Love slain and rise again victorious he knew that he witnessed, in a figure, the consummation of all things, the Bridal of all Bridals, the mystery that is beyond all mysteries, accomplished from the foundation of the world. So day by day the house of his life became more magical.

And at the same time he began to guess that if in the New Life there are new and unheard-of joys, there are also new and unheard-of dangers. In his manuscript books which professed to deliver the outer sense of those mysterious "Hidden Songs of Job Sant" there was a little chapter that bore the heading: *Fons Sacer non in communem Vsum convertendus est,* and by diligence, with much use of the grammar and dictionary, Darnell was able to construe the by no means complex Latin of his ancestor. The special book which contained the chapter in question was one of the most singular in the collection, since it bore the title *Terra de Iolo,* and on the surface, with an ingenious concealment of its real symbolism, it affected to give an account of the orchards, fields, woods, roads, tenements, and waterways in the possession of Darnell's ancestors. Here, then, he read of the Holy Well, hidden in the Wistman's Wood — *Sylva Sapientum* — "a fountain of abundant water, which no heats of summer can ever dry, which no flood can ever defile, which is as a water of life, to them that thirst for life, a stream of cleansing to them that would be pure, and a medicine of such healing virtue that by it, through the might of God and the intercession of His saints, the most grievous wounds are made whole."

But the water of this well was to be kept sacred perpetually, it was not to be used for any common purpose, nor to satisfy any bodily thirst; but ever to be esteemed as holy, "even as the water which the priest hath hallowed." And in the margin a comment in a later hand taught Darnell something of the meaning of these prohibitions. He was warned not to use the Well of Life as a mere luxury of mortal life, as a new sensation, as a means of making the insipid cup of everyday existence more palatable. "For," said the commentator, "we are not called to sit as the spectators in a theater, there to watch the play performed before us, but we are rather summoned to stand in the very scene itself, and there fervently to enact our parts in a great and wonderful mystery."

Darnell could quite understand the temptation that was thus indicated. Though he had gone but a little way on the path, and had barely tested the overrunnings of that mystic well, he was already aware of the enchantment that was transmuting all the world about him, informing his life with a strange significance and romance. London seemed a city of the Arabian Nights, and its labyrinths of streets an enchanted maze; its long avenues of lighted lamps were as starry systems, and its immensity became for him an image of the endless universe. He could well imagine how pleasant it might be to linger in such a world as this, to sit apart and dream, beholding the strange pageant played before him; but the Sacred Well was not for common use, it was for the cleansing of the soul, and the healing of the grievous wounds of the spirit. There must be yet another transformation: London had become Baghdad; it must at last be transmuted to Syon, or in the phrase of one of his old documents, the City of the Cup.

And there were yet darker perils which the Iolo MSS. (as his father had named the collection) hinted at more or less obscurely. There were suggestions of an awful region which the soul might enter, of a transmutation that was unto death, of evocations which could summon the utmost forces of evil from their dark places — in a word, of that sphere which is represented to most of us under the crude and somewhat childish symbolism of Black Magic. And here again he was not altogether without a dim comprehension of what was meant. He found himself recalling an odd incident that had happened long ago, which had remained all the years in his mind unheeded, amongst the many insignificant recollections of his childhood, and now rose before him, clear and distinct and full of meaning. It was on that memorable visit to the old house in the west, and the whole scene returned, with its smallest events, and the voices seemed to sound in his ears. It was a grey, still day of heavy heat that he remembered: he had stood on the lawn after breakfast, and wondered at the great peace and silence of the world. Not a leaf stirred in the trees on the lawn, not a whisper came

from the myriad leaves of the wood; the flowers gave
out sweet and heavy odors as if they breathed the
dreams of the summer night; and far down the valley,
the winding river was like dim silver under that dim
and silvery sky, and the far hills and woods and fields
vanished in the mist. The stillness of the air held him
as with a charm; he leant all the morning against the
rails that parted the lawn from the meadow, breathing
the mystic breath of summer, and watching the fields
brighten as with a sudden blossoming of shining flowers as the high mist grew thin for a moment before the
hidden sun. As he watched thus, a man weary with
heat, with some glance of horror in his eyes, passed
him on his way to the house; but he stayed at his post
till the old bell in the turret rang, and they dined all
together, masters and servants, in the dark cool room
that looked toward the still leaves of the wood. He
could see that his uncle was upset about something,
and when they had finished dinner he heard him tell
his father that there was trouble at a farm; and it was
settled that they should all drive oven in the afternoon
to some place with a strange name. But when the time
came Mr. Darnell was too deep in old books and
tobacco smoke to be stirred from his corner, and
Edward and his uncle went alone in the dogcart. They
drove swiftly down the narrow lane, into the road that
followed the winding river, and crossed the bridge at
Caermaen by the moldering Roman walls, and then,
skirting the deserted, echoing village, they came out on
a broad white turnpike road, and the limestone dust
followed them like a cloud. Then, suddenly, they
turned to the north by such a road as Edward had never
seen before. It was so narrow that there was barely room
for the cart to pass, and the footway was of rock, and
the banks rose high above them as they slowly climbed
the long, steep way, and the untrimmed hedges on

either side shut out the light. And the ferns grew thick and green upon the banks, and hidden wells dripped down upon them; and the old man told him how the lane in winter was a torrent of swirling water, so that no one could pass by it. On they went, ascending and then again descending, always in that deep hollow under the wild woven boughs, and the boy wondered vainly what the country was like on either side. And now the air grew darker, and the hedge on one bank was but the verge of a dark and rustling wood, and the grey limestone rocks had changed to dark-red earth flecked with green patches and veins of marl, and suddenly in the stillness from the depths of the wood a bind began to sing a melody that charmed the heart into another world, that sang to the child's soul of the blessed færy realm beyond the woods of the earth, where the wounds of man are healed. And so at last, after many turnings and windings, they came to a high bare land where the lane broadened out into a kind of common, and along the edge of this place there were scattered three or four old cottages, and one of them was a little tavern. Here they stopped, and a man came out and tethered the tired horse to a post and gave him water; and old Mr. Darnell took the child's hand and led him by a path across the fields. The boy could see the country now, but it was all a strange, undiscovered land; they were in the heart of a wilderness of hills and valleys that he had never looked upon, and they were going down a wild, steep hillside, where the narrow path wound in and out amidst gorse and towering bracken, and the sun gleaming out for a moment, there was a gleam of white water far below in a narrow valley, where a little brook poured and rippled from stone to stone. They went down the hill, and through a brake, and then, hidden in dark-green orchards, they came upon a long, low whitewashed house, with a stone roof strangely colored by the growth of moss and lichens. Mr. Darnell knocked at a heavy oaken door, and they came into a dim room where but little light entered through the thick glass in the deep-set window. There were heavy beams in the ceiling, and a great fireplace sent out an odor of burning wood that Darnell never forgot, and the room seemed to him full of women who talked all together in frightened tones. Mr. Darnell beckoned to a tall, grey old man, who wore corduroy knee-breeches, and the boy, sitting on a high straight-backed chair, could see the old man and his uncle passing to and fro across the windowpanes, as they walked together on the garden path. The women stopped their talk for a moment, and one of them brought him a glass of milk and an apple from some cold inner chamber; and then, suddenly, from a room above there rang out a shrill and terrible shriek, and then, in a young girl's voice, a more terrible song. It was not like anything the child had ever heard, but as the man recalled it to his memory, he knew to what song it might be compared — to a certain chant indeed that summons the angels and archangels to assist in the great Sacrifice. But as this song chants of the heavenly army, so did that seem to summon all the hierarchy of evil, the hosts of Lilith and Samael; and the words that rang out with such awful modulations — *neumata inferorum* — were in some unknown tongue that few men have even heard on earth.

The women glared at one another with horror in their eyes, and he saw one or two of the oldest of them clumsily making an old sign upon their breasts. Then they began to speak again, and he remembered fragments of their talk.

"She has been up there," said one, pointing vaguely oven her shoulder.

"She'd never know the way," answered another.

"They be all gone that went there."

"There be naught there in these days."

"How can you tell that, Gwenllian? 'Tis not for us to say that."

"My great-grandmother did know some that had been there," said a very old woman. "She told me how they was taken afterward."

And then his uncle appeared at the door, and they went their way as they had come. Edward Darnell never heard anymore of it, non whether the girl died or recovered from her strange attack; but the scene had haunted his mind in boyhood, and now the recollection of it came to him with a certain note of warning, as a symbol of dangers that might be in the way.

*I*t would be impossible to carry on the history of Edward Darnell and of Mary his wife to a greater length, since from this point their legend is full of impossible events, and seems to put on the semblance of the stories of the Graal. It is certain, indeed, that in this world they changed their lives, like King Arthur, but this is a work which no chronicler has cared to describe with any amplitude of detail. Darnell, it is true, made a little book, partly consisting of queer verse which might have been written by an inspired infant, and partly made up of "notes and exclamations" in an odd dog-Latin which he had picked up from the "Iolo MSS.," but it is to be feared that this work, even if published in its entirety, would cast but little light on a perplexing story. He called this piece of literature "In Exitu Israel," and wrote on the title page the motto, doubtless of his own composition, *"Nunc certe scio quod omnia legenda; omnes historiæ, omnes fabulæ, omnis Scriptura sint de ME narrata."* It is only too evident that his

Latin was not learnt at the feet of Cicero; but in this dialect he relates the great history of the "New Life" as it was manifested to him. The "poems" are even stranger. One, headed (with an odd reminiscence of old-fashioned books) "Lines written on looking down from a Height in London on a Board School suddenly lit up by the Sun" begins thus: —

One day when I was all alone
I found a wondrous little stone,
It lay forgotten on the road
Far from the ways of man's abode.
When on this stone mine eyes I cast
I saw my Treasure found at last.
I pressed it hard against my face,
I covered it with my embrace,
I hid it in a secret place.
And every day I went to see
This stone that was my ecstasy;
And worshipped it with flowers rare,
And secret words and sayings fair.
O stone, so rare and red and wise
O fragment of far Paradise,
O Star, whose light is life! O Sea,
Whose ocean is infinity!
Thou art a fire that ever burns,
And all the world to wonder turns;
And all the dust of the dull day
By thee is changed and purged away,
So that, where'er I look, I see
A world of a Great Majesty.
The sullen river rolls all gold,
The desert park's a færy wold,
When on the trees the wind is borne
I hear the sound of Arthur's horn
I see no town of grim grey ways,

But a great city all ablaze
With burning torches, to light up
The pinnacles that shrine the Cup.
Ever the magic wine is poured,
Ever the Feast shines on the board,
Ever the song is borne on high
That chants the holy Magistry —
Etc. etc. etc.

From such documents as these it is clearly impossible to gather any very definite information. But on the last page Darnell has written —

"So I awoke from a dream of a London suburb, of daily labor, of weary, useless little things; and as my eyes were opened I saw that I was in an ancient wood, where a clear well rose into grey film and vapor beneath a misty, glimmering heat. And a form came toward me from the hidden places of the wood, and my love and I were united by the well."

www.ingramcontent.com/pod-product-compliance
Lightning Source LLC
Chambersburg PA
CBHW050803250626
47155CB00005B/2191